Bridge of Time

BRIDGE
OF TIME

LEWIS BUZBEE

FEIWEL AND FRIENDS

NEW YORK

A FEIWEL AND FRIENDS BOOK
An Imprint of Macmillan

Library of Congress Cataloging-in-Publication Data Available

ISBN: 978-0-312-38257-5

Feiwel and Friends logo designed by Filomena Tuosto

First Edition: 2012

1   3   5   7   9   10   8   6   4   2

mackids.com

FOR
LIZ SZABLA,
SAN FRANCISCAN

The side-excursions are the life of our life-voyage,
and should be, also, of its history.

— MARK TWAIN

An Awful Morning – Weird Kitchen – Worst Field Trip Ever – Bullies on the Bus – A Missing Friend

What Lee Jones should have suspected when he entered the City School's multipurpose room was that the most awful morning of his life was about to get much awfuller. But Lee made a mistake that's far too common. Brushing his hair before school, Lee convinced himself that his life was so horrid already, it couldn't possibly get worse. Right?

Not necessarily.

Let's back up a bit and see precisely how awful Lee's life was that morning before it took a turn for the worse.

In less than a month, Lee would graduate from the eighth grade, all in all a good thing. He was excited to start high school, yet was a little nervous, too. Even though he'd be staying at the City School, only moving from the fourth floor to the fifth, and even though he knew a lot of the high school kids already, freshman year was a bit of a mystery to him. Going to high school seemed like entering a big dark cave through a narrow tunnel. You could get lost in there and never find your way out. But this was a minor awfulness for Lee, the usual sort of stuff you face in life. Not great but doable.

The true awfulness about starting high school was that Lee would be going into that dark cave alone. His very best friend—and pretty much only friend these days—Joan Lee, was transferring to Starr King Prep in the fall. Joan and Lee had attended the City School together since pre-K, but it wasn't until sixth grade, on the first day of middle school, that they became best friends.

That day, both of them running late because neither could open their lockers, they found themselves next to each other in the hot lunch line in the basement cafeteria. As they pushed their trays along, they talked about their stupid lockers and the new teachers and last summer and were there going to be real dances and were eighth graders as cruel as they were supposed to be.

When they arrived at the dessert station, however, both Lee and Joan reached for the same Rice Krispies square, which happened to be the last Rice Krispies square. Joan held one side of the white plastic plate, Lee the other, and they commenced debating over who had dibs. Joan suggested that since she was first in line, the Rice Krispies square was hers. Lee claimed he only let Joan go first because he was a gentleman, so Joan should repay his good manners by letting him have the Rice Krispies square. Joan said she never asked him to be so polite; Lee said he couldn't help himself. Joan tugged at the plate; Lee tugged back.

Later, they sometimes wonder if they would have become friends or not if they *had* shared that last Rice Krispies square. Maybe if they had broken the square in two, middle school would have turned out different. Lee would have taken his half, Joan hers, and they would have gone their separate ways.

But that possibility never had a chance to arrive. Because right at that moment, Trevor McGahee, the biggest sixth grader in the history of sixth graders, reached between Joan and Lee, snatched that Rice Krispies square off the white plastic plate, and proceeded to lick it with his big gross tongue. Trevor had claimed his dessert. Welcome to middle school. Ew.

Joan and Lee each let go of the plate, then looked at

each other, then gave each other THE SHUDDER. Both of them shook a little, both raised their shoulders a little, both made a disgusted expression, and both let out low moans. This was the first time they shared what they would later call a LOOK. Joan and Lee soon discovered they could carry on an entire conversation with one shared glance, one simple LOOK. If it hadn't been for that last Rice Krispies square and for big dumb gross Trevor, they might never have known that.

Joan and Lee did eat lunch together that day and started hanging out all the time—no big deal. They still had their other friends, but in middle school, they found that friendships and alliances changed on a weekly, if not daily basis. Oh, the other kids gave them a hard time, a boy and girl being best friends and all, but since this was middle school, the other kids would get bored quickly and move on to giving some other kids some other hard time about something else. Joan and Lee developed a LOOK to cover all this, THE MIDDLE SCHOOL, which roughly translated as, "Hey, it's middle school, whacha gonna do?"

Their friendship was not a perfect one, but true friendships never were, Lee figured. What often helped build a friendship were the differences between the two friends, and Joan and Lee were opposites in many ways. Lee, Joan would probably say, was a little too laid-back, a little too "Whatever, dude." Joan, Lee would happily tell you, was wound up way too tight, a homework-eating-robot machine. They were perfectly mismatched. Even their names said this, mirror images that were also opposites—Lee Jones, Joan Lee.

But despite their differences, maybe because of them, they both knew that their friendship was THE ONLY THING that made the murky swamp of middle school possible. All those cliques and romance dramas and popularity death matches—ugh!

But now Joan was leaving. Her parents had developed "serious reservations" about the City School's "commitment to calculus" and were switching her to Starr King. Joan refused to ask her parents to change their minds. She would stand up to anybody in the world, Lee knew, except her parents. And no matter how much Lee's parents told him that Joan's transfer was "best for everyone," and no matter how much he and Joan made promises to stay FRIENDS FOREVER, Lee suspected that such promises were impossible to keep. Deep down he feared that come the fall, he would never see Joan again. Their lives would be even more different than they were now.

Joan lived in San Francisco's Presidio Heights, which is a very posh neighborhood, and Lee lived in the great flat streets of the city's Sunset District, a neighborhood not known for its poshness. Joan's enormous house looked out over the Presidio, the bay and the Golden Gate Bridge; Lee's house looked out over Eighth Avenue and May Lee's Free Chinese Delivery.

Where the City School was packed into a five-story sardine can downtown, Starr King Prep sprawled over acres of playing field above Ocean Beach. The schools' athletic teams even played in different leagues, so he and Joan wouldn't see each other at games. As an unspoken rule, Starr Kings and City Schoolers did not hang out together. It was highly unlikely that Lee and Joan would "run into" each other, no matter how often their parents told them otherwise. The size of the world was going to push them apart.

But Joan transferring was not the awfullest of the awful things this foggy May morning. The most awful thing about this morning had arrived just the night before at dinner. It arrived with a sudden, sickening quiet and some very strange behavior on the part of Lee's kitchen.

He and his parents were sitting at the kitchen table, and Lee was just about to tear into a big and juicy BLT, when his mom began to speak ever so softly. The softness in her voice should have been Lee's first clue, but BLTs can be distracting.

"Honey," his mom said, "your father and I have, well . . ."

Lee set down his sandwich. Everything seemed to stop. He looked over his dad's shoulder out the kitchen window. He could see the sky there, it was a foggy evening, and he knew the world outside that window was still going on, cars and buses and planes and dinners and all the rest. But here in this kitchen, everything had stopped. Lee's father stared at his own BLT; his mother held a glass of water to her lips; the lamp above the table hung empty and airless. Then, very clearly, as if she were actually there, Lee saw Joan's face pop up in the kitchen window. She and Lee exchanged a big old WHAT NOW?

His mom spoke again; time tripped forward.

"Your father and I," she said, looking straight at Lee, "we've decided that it's best for everyone that he and I get a divorce."

The first thing Lee thought was, Whenever you hear an adult use the phrase "best for everyone," you should run as far and fast as possible. The second thing he thought was, A divorce, really? Then the kitchen did that funny thing again, and everything seemed to stop. Well, Lee stopped, but his parents went on.

For what might have been hours, Lee and his

parents sat at the kitchen table, *not* eating their BLTs, that's how weird it was. Lee sat; his parents talked. They wanted, they said, to help him understand, make him know that everything would be all right and nothing would change. They went over everything again and again—"the time had come," "drifted apart," "things change," "things won't change," "a shock they knew," "only to be expected."

It didn't matter what they said because Lee was still wandering around in the moment when his mom first said it was "best for everyone" and "divorce." His parents were going forward in time, Lee could tell, but he was stranded in the past, where he was just about to bite into his BLT and the word "divorce" had never been spoken.

So Lee nodded and hmmmed and yessed and told his parents he understood, and that he was all right. That was some other Lee listening to them, some future Lee.

Some part of Lee eventually moved forward; he went to his room and did his homework and got ready for bed. All he really wanted to do was call Joan, but that was not allowed after dinner, part of his "homework contract." And so he did what any self-respecting eighth-grade boy would do at such a moment. He went to sleep.

The next morning, however, neither homework nor sleep could keep Lee stuck in the past where life was still good and his parents were not getting a divorce. While he brushed his hair in front of the bathroom mirror, the crushing truth of the present punched him hard in the gut—his parents were getting a divorce?! He was flooded with a rush of feelings—rage and fists, sorrow and tears, and something that was like laughter, the kind of laughter that just won't stop and scares you.

Lee tried hard to make his life flash before his eyes, to recall all the great family memories he knew he possessed. But nothing would come—no picnics in Golden Gate Park or at Ocean Beach, no long afternoons in the backyard with his parents barbecuing and reading, no movie nights and all that popcorn, no nothing. He could not get to the past, where everything was the way it was supposed to be. There was just now, staring into the mirror and the sickening fact that his parents . . .

Lee had to get out of this house. He did his best to push the whole stupid divorce thing down and down. He ate breakfast and rode to school with his parents—who would just not stop talking—and all the while he concentrated on the two very good things that would happen that day.

First, and most important, he would get to talk to Joan about this whole silly divorce business—what were his parents thinking? They were perfectly happy;

everyone knew that. It always helped to talk to Joan, even when they were talking about nothing.

Second, they would be doing this talking at California Dreaming, their favorite amusement park in the universe. Today was Eighth Grade Getaway Day, and the park would be filled with graduating middle schoolers from all over the Bay Area. Lee and Joan had promised each other that NO MATTER WHAT they were going to ride the Vortex this year. Seriously.

So, unfortunately, Lee was feeling pretty good when his parents dropped him off at school, and without the tiniest good-bye to them, he melted into the stream of students that flowed through the City School's front doors. Today had to be better.

Joan wouldn't be at school yet, she was always late, so Lee snagged their usual place, a window seat on top of the shelves where the board games were kept. This was where Lee and Joan had been sitting all of eighth grade—off to the side, on the edge of things, removed from the larger herd. They sat in the back row at assemblies, in the far corner of the lunch yard, and high in the visitors' bleachers at basketball games.

It's not that they were antisocial or anything, they just didn't like being crushed by all the squealing and crying and manic text messages. All that gossip—you could have it. Besides, they agreed, the view from the edge of the herd was so much better, so much more to see and talk about there. Off to the side, that was their world.

Lee saved their spots and watched the herd at work. You didn't have to be a genius to know this was a field-trip day—the running, the screaming, the laughing, uck, that smell. Even more so, there was a vibe in the air that said, "We are outta here!"

Mr. Ruszel, Lee's homeroom teacher (but otherwise a pretty cool guy) stood before the assembly and clapped five times: One! Two! Three, four, five! Like well-trained lab rats, the students clapped in response, then fell quiet.

"Okay," Mr. Ruszel said, taking a deep breath. "Here's the good news."

No, not that, not "the good news." Starting with "the good news" was never good. Right up there with "best for everyone."

The good news was that there would still be a Get-away Day. Lee's stomach dropped far and fast, and not in a fun, oh-my-God, roller-coaster kind of way.

The bad news? They were *not* going to California Dreaming. There had been a mix-up with the deposit check.

The sound of sixty-seven eighth graders being cruelly disappointed all at once might be spelled something like this: "Awwwwww-ooooooohhhhh-oooo-aiiiiii!" But spelling really can't make a word as loud and terrifying as the sound that now swallowed MPR4. Imagine the sound of a jet plane—an angry, sulky jet plane—landing in your living room.

Now, Lee thought, this is as low as it goes. Can't get no lower nohow.

You should never think that, never, not out loud or to yourself.

The field trip, Mr. Ruszel said, their one and only, once-in-a-lifetime Eighth Grade Getaway Day had been changed to . . . Fort Point. To understand the horror of this choice, it helps if you've attended school in San Francisco. Fort Point is a Civil War–era, well, fort, which sits under one end of the Golden Gate Bridge. It was, Lee admitted, a pretty cool place, but he and the other eighth graders in MPR4 had probably been there a combined total of a million times. And Fort Point was no California Dreaming, especially on a foggy May day like today. They would freeze to death.

It took Mr. Ruszel about nine years to get everyone quiet and moving. Lee let himself be pushed along the halls and down the stairs, then he darted for the second bus. Always take the second bus, Lee and Joan had come to agree. It's the safest bus, less crowded.

He grabbed an aisle seat, to save the window for

Joan. She would pop up any minute, he knew, apologizing profusely. They had a lot to talk about. At least that, at least Joan would be here.

But she wasn't popping up. And she had better pop up soon. If you missed a bus for a field trip, you had to spend all day in the library, by yourself—without computer access!

The bus's engine growled to life—no Joan. And then Trevor McGahee's face appeared over the seat in front of Lee. It was not a pretty face, to be sure. Apparently, Trevor had not got the memo about the second bus being the safer one. Or maybe he had.

"Move your butt, loser," Trevor said with a sneer he practiced in the mirror every morning. "Your loser girlfriend's not coming. We're taking that seat." Trevor and his goons—his goons were always right behind him—laughed.

The bus actually pulled away—without Joan. Trevor's goons squished Lee against the window.

TWO

Cold but Right – A Weird
Dining Room – Quadruple Jinx –
Cattle to the Slaughter

It was the principle of the thing! Joan Lee, alone in the foggy, freezing parking lot of the Fort Point National Historic Site, stood as far away from the warmth of her mother's BMW as she could get. All on a matter of principle. You had to stand up for your principles, Joan believed. This was actually her most important principle: Always stand up for your principles. Joan hadn't known until this morning, however, that standing up for your principles could make you so cold.

But once Joan got up a head of steam on a matter of principle, she wasn't about to give in. And the principle that had her freezing right now was too important: Her parents were being huge butt faces, and no way was she ever going to speak to them again, ever.

Joan was glad she had her principles; she only wished she'd brought a warmer coat. As if the heated interior of her mother's BMW were calling her name, Joan turned that way. Her mother was making some dorky fluttery gesture with her hands. She was only urging Joan to please get in the car, but it was embarrassing, nonetheless. As if the seagulls on the rocks might care.

Joan turned away from the obviously toasty car. There was stupid old Fort Point, obviously freezing. The bay next to it, obviously freezing, too. And above them, the Golden Gate Bridge, which was always freezing, even on the sunniest day. Joan was alone in the parking lot and shivering—all because of her stupid principles.

She wasn't surprised by the fact that her parents had decided to get a divorce, not at all. Her parents were always fighting. No, Joan was angry at them because they had left her out of the loop, and Joan hated being left out of any loop.

Her parents had waited to tell her about the divorce until after dinner the night before, right as her favorite dessert, tapioca, was set on the table. They had waited until her brothers and sisters already knew and were now conveniently out of the house. They had waited until the divorce papers were signed and filed. They had waited to tell Joan, "the baby," until it was too late.

"It's time that you know," her father said. "Your mother and I are getting a divorce."

The dining room went all weird and wonky. Her father smoothed a linen napkin across his lap; her mother lifted her tea cup without sipping from it. Her parents stayed there like that, frozen in place at the far end of the suddenly enormous dining-room table.

Only Joan moved forward, rocketing ahead in time, seeing everything as it would be after the divorce. The arguments that were sure to continue, the two "homes," the two bedrooms, the two parents, her mother crying more, and her father more quiet than ever. Horrible holidays.

The divorce sent a huge crack right down the middle of Joan's future, and everywhere she looked into that future, she saw herself leaping from one side of the crack to the other—her father's side, her mother's side. Eventually, the crack would widen too much for her to leap across. In the future, she knew, she would fall into that crack.

Her father spoke again from where he was frozen in the past, and Joan looped back to her parents in the dining room.

"Yes," he said, "I will be moving out of the house tomorrow. Your mother and I feel this is best for everyone, and we want you to know that nothing else will change. Life will go on as before."

Her father looked down at his bowl of tapioca.

"Do you have any questions?" her mother asked. Her stupid teacup just hung there in midair, and once again, Joan raced off into the future, leaving her parents behind.

No, Joan had no questions. But she did have a whole bunch of answers, which she saw clearly from her new position in the future.

Her father would dutifully pick up Joan every Friday night—her siblings would all be busy—for an awkward dinner at some fancy restaurant, which would be followed by an awkward weekend at her father's new place, which would probably smell funny. All of this would be followed by the longest Sunday evening in the history of the world. Then one day, her father would introduce Joan to a new woman she never ever wanted to meet.

Her mother would buy Joan lots of presents, expensive little presents she'd leave on her pillow, earrings or a new cell phone. Then there would be tears, lots of them, and Joan would have to feel guilty about everything. The house would be quiet, and her mother would always be alone.

Joan's oldest brother, Ben, would graduate from college, move out of the house, and disappear into some city of the future. Her other brother, Newton, would get into his souped-up Honda Civic and drive around San Francisco all night, tires squealing. Her oldest sister, Alice, would be surrounded by even more boys than she was now, a flock of boys with bad haircuts and dopey expressions. And her other sister, Fiona, would never come home from volleyball practices and tournaments.

Joan would study and study and ace her PSATs and her SATs and her APs. She'd study so much, people would only ever see the back of her head.

There was not one single thing about this future that Joan liked. Not even the presents.

But what she hated most about this future? There was no Lee. It was lonely in the future. If Joan could just catch one glimpse of Lee out here, share one big old NO WAY! with him, the future might seem doable.

Joan tried to yell all these answers to her parents, but where they were stuck, at that dining-room table in the past, was too far away. No matter how loud she yelled, they did not hear her and nothing changed. And believe it, Joan was yelling real loud, louder than a goose at a barn dance.

"Young lady," her father said, raising his voice. "You must lower your voice."

Joan was sucked back to the present, which was now her past.

Her parents had heard nothing.

"Fine," Joan said. "I see. Good luck to you both."

She raced to her room, zipping up the stairs and crashing down the hall. The door flew shut behind her.

All she really wanted to do at that moment was call or text Lee. A call would be better; his voice. But she would have to wait until tomorrow. Lee's parents cut him off electronically after dinner. It was straight to homework, and only homework, for Lee then.

Fine, no big deal. They would talk tomorrow morning and then keep talking. Joan had already decided—on principle!—that Lee was the only human she would ever speak to again.

So there was only one thing left to do—homework. Joan didn't need to clear off her desk; it was always spotless. She opened her laptop, pulled the first book off the priority-arranged stack in the top-right corner of the desk, and got down to it.

By the time she finished with algebra for the night,

she had advanced three weeks into the syllabus, way ahead of even snotty old Darrin. By the time she turned off her computer, closed her books, called it a night, she had worked up through the Renaissance in history/geography and was twelve chapters ahead in *Great Expectations*.

The next morning, the house was its usual chaos, brothers and sisters flying everywhere, constant screeching, all hurry-hurry and no progress. Every morning was the same; every morning Joan was late. But not this morning—she wouldn't stand for it. Not with Getaway Day here—that was a bus Joan was not going to miss.

She scooped up her prepacked backpack, swallowed some toast, then stood by the door to the garage, and glowered at her mother. Joan did not speak to her—on principle!—but just swung her backpack from side to side, kicking it with her knees. Finally, her mother got the message.

This morning her mother was driving with unusual caution, actually stopping at stop signs. Hurry, please, Joan wanted to yell, but didn't—on principle!

"Do you want to talk some more?" her mother asked in a soft faraway voice. "About last night? Because you—"

"Ma," Joan said. "Drive, please. It's Getaway Day. Don't make me miss it."

Okay, that, right there, that was the *very* last thing she would ever say to her mother.

If possible, Joan's mother was driving even slower now. If she drove any slower, Joan thought, they'd be going backwards.

Of course, they were late for school *and* for the bus. But it hardly mattered that they were late. No California Dreaming? Fort Point? You've got to be kidding. It was Florence at the front desk who delivered the dire news.

The buses had already left for Fort Point, and with Joan's mom driving slower than she had ever driven in her life, Joan was certain they would never catch up. But weirdly, the BMW arrived at Fort Point before the buses. First late, then early. Something had happened to time in the dining room last night.

So, here she was, freezing and *not* going to California Dreaming. She was standing in the parking lot of Fort Point and pretty much hating everything. Even her principles.

At least, there was Lee. She would tell him everything, and he would listen and understand and ask all the right questions. This was what Lee did best—among the many cool things about him. He listened.

When the buses finally appeared on the seawall road, Joan's mother started up the BMW and pulled away. Joan did not even bother to look at her—a matter of principle.

The kids streamed off the buses, looking surprisingly happy for *not* being at California Dreaming. Joan spotted Lee at the back of the second bus, where he was pushed up against a window, surrounded by Trevor and his goons, but he managed to squeeze past them.

She knew exactly what she was going to say to him—she'd been practicing it in her head.

"You'll never believe it," Lee was yelling. He stomped towards her through the crowd. "My parents are getting a divorce!"

Joan was a little confused. First, Lee was never like this, so loud, so . . . stompy. Second, she thought that maybe she and Lee had switched places in the night. *His* parents were getting a divorce? Did he just say that? No, *her* parents were getting a divorce.

"Your parents?" she said. "My parents, too. They're getting a divorce."

"No way!" they both said, right into each other's faces.

"Way!" they both said.

The other students streamed away from them, blurs of blue and pink and yellow and teal. Joan stared at Lee, who was staring at her. They were both smiling, and suddenly she was on the verge of laughing, because of all the smiling. This was one of the main reasons Lee was her best friend. Lee got how weird things could be. If this had been some other friend, especially some other girl, it would be all about the drama. But with Lee, it was all about the weirdness.

"Okay," she said. "When did you find out?"

"Last night," he said, his smile dangerously wide. "At dinner."

"Me, too."

"No way!" they both said.

"Way!" they both said.

"Wow," Lee said. "Talk about a jinx. That's gotta be a quadruple jinx. We must owe everyone in the world a Coke."

Though normally Joan would have punched Lee on the arm at a time like this—that is, when she thought he was being cool—she surprised herself by reaching out and hugging him. Very casually, of course.

"Okay, people, let's get a move on. History awaits." Mr. Ruszel herded the crowd into the dark sallyport tunnel that was the main entrance to Fort Point.

Joan was thinking, Cattle, sort of like cattle being led somewhere. Slaughter or safety? Boredom or adventure?

Maybe this was a magic tunnel, part of an elaborate Getaway Day hoax. Maybe there was a fantastical world at the other end.

Joan tugged at Lee's elbow and dragged him to the back of the herd, where they could talk more freely. Joan had done this field trip too many times already; no need to pay attention today.

THREE

The Wonders of History – On the Coldness of Brick – The Great Escape – Lunch, a Lighthouse, and a Nap

While history was normally one of Lee's favorite subjects, this morning the "wonders of history," as the park ranger kept saying, were lost on him.

It was hard to concentrate on Fort Point and its "colorful Civil War past" when you were freezing down to the very marrow of your bones. It was no surprise that San Francisco was cold in May; May was the start of fog season. And Fort Point, being an old brick building right next to the bay, at the very spot where the fog enters and exits the bay, well, cold at Fort Point in May is inevitable.

But Lee—and everyone else from the City School—had not dressed for Fort Point in May. They'd dressed for California Dreaming, which was fifty miles south, in Santa Clara, where it was guaranteed to be in the eighties.

So no one had brought real jackets or dressed in layers. Lee wore a lightweight hoodie his mom had insisted on, "just in case," but he was still shivering. Joan had nothing but a denim vest over a T-shirt. She held herself tightly, and Lee could actually hear her teeth chattering.

Everyone appeared as pitiful as Lee felt. The eighth-grade class of the City School stood in the center of Fort Point's main courtyard, surrounded on all sides by three floors of brick walls and archways. The wind swirled and punched.

Ranger Rhonda, in her green uniform and Smokey the Bear hat, was going on about the "wonders of history." She had no idea that the only reason this group of eighth graders was still and silent this morning was because their blood had iced over. Her audience wasn't so much captive as paralyzed.

Ranger Rhonda tapped on her paper-laden clipboard.

"In 1861 the barbette tier—or what you civilians know as the top level, or *roof*, of the fort—sported eleven thirty-two pounders, eight eight-inch Columbiads, and two ten-inch Columbusses."

Ranger Rhonda continued to consult her clipboard

for facts, which she fired over the heads of the students like, well, cannonballs from a cannon. In the twelve trillion times Lee had been to Fort Point, he'd heard at least six billion different rangers, and he knew Ranger Rhonda, or at least her type. History, to Ranger Rhonda, was a series of facts that only she possessed.

What Lee liked most about history weren't the facts, but the lives that happened between and around those facts. He'd always enjoyed imagining, when he'd been to Fort Point before, what it was like for the soldiers who'd been stationed here in the 1860s, or the Spanish soldiers who built a tiny adobe outpost here in the 1700s. What did the world look like to these people? How did they spend their days? What did they talk about? What, Lee wanted to know, was the first thought that entered the head of a Union solider, a boy thousands of miles from home, when he woke up in the morning? And how did he stay warm?

"And this visitor," Ranger Rhonda was saying, "actually confused 'hotshot' with a mortar shell. A nineteenth-century soldier would *never* make such a mistake."

Never, Lee thought? Never ever? Not once?

Joan dug her elbow into Lee's ribs.

"Let's get out of here," she said. "We need to talk."

Lee gazed at his "Guns of Fort Point" brochure, while he spoke to Joan. This was an old trick of his. In a class or on a field trip, anywhere where you were supposed to be paying attention, if you pretended to read something, you could talk more freely. The teacher—or ranger—apparently thought you were one of those students who had to move his lips while he read. It was a great cover.

"Two seconds," he said. "She's just about to send us on a scavenger hunt. I've been through this one before. After they show us the cannons, we've got to go looking for the places they would have been mounted. We'll get away then. Are they really getting divorced?"

"Yep."

"Man."

"Okay," Ranger Rhonda trilled, "let's buddy up and go find those armaments. Experience the wonders of history. And meet back here in ten minutes. Oh, remember, stay on the first level for now. Don't want you to get lost."

"C'mon," Lee said. He grabbed Joan's hand and pulled her away.

Joan planted her feet.

"Where?"

Lee had no idea. So he made one up.

"To the top," he said. "We'll be alone."

Joan held back for a moment; Lee tugged at her hand.

"Oh, look, the lovebirds." It was Trevor again, breathing his gross breath all over them. What exactly was his problem, except that he was a butt face?

Lee looked at Joan, rolled his eyes.

Joan tugged on Lee's hand.

"Trevor," she said, "look, a blimp!" And when Trevor turned to look—duh!—Joan and Lee ran to the far corner of the courtyard and up the three flights of granite spiral stairs to the roof of Fort Point.

They were all alone on top of the fort. From the first-floor courtyard, Lee could hear the screams and shouts of the scavenger hunt below. Above them, the Golden Gate Bridge, with its constant stream of cars and trucks, straddled Fort Point like a gigantic orange spider. But the fog was so thick, nothing else was visible. Not the city, not the Presidio, not Marin across the bay, not Alcatraz, not the ships undoubtedly passing close by. The bridge itself disappeared, dissolved in the fog, a bridge that led to nowhere. This was the perfect place to be.

Joan ran ahead to the ocean side of the fort and hunkered down against the brick wall of a cannon bay. Lee squatted next to her, and they pressed themselves against the wall, out of the wind. But Lee was still freezing, possibly even more so. It was the bricks. For over

150 years these bricks had been exposed to the cold and damp of San Francisco Bay. All 150 years of that cold now transferred into Lee's body.

"So," he said, "what do you want to talk about? I mean . . . I don't know what I mean."

The brick was so cold, his brain had frozen.

"I can't talk. I'm too cold." Joan spoke into her hands.

"I know."

"Brick."

"Cold."

"Help."

"Maybe we should go back down," Lee said. It hurt to say a sentence that long.

"Lighthouse," Joan whispered.

Then she was off, sprinting towards the stubby white lighthouse that rose two stories above the court-yard and looked out over the vast Pacific. Lee had always wanted to climb the metal stairs to the lighthouse, but the little chain and its DO NOT ENTER sign had kept him out.

Joan stood next to the lighthouse stairs.

"Come on," she said. "Let's go in. It's got to be warmer."

"But what if the door's locked?" he said.

"We'll come back down?"

"But," Lee said, looking around. "We're not supposed to."

Joan gave him THE STARE, a look as cold as all the cold bricks in Fort Point.

"We're not supposed to be up here, either," she said, "but here we are."

"But—"

Here came THE STARE again.

"Lee," was all she said.

Funny thing about Joan. Lee often had to be the one to commit the first trespass. Joan was often too stubborn—or scared—to take the first step. But once she made that step, well, watch out!

A few months ago, they'd messed up Trevor's locker, and it had been, at first, Lee's idea. Lee and Joan were supposed to be in study hall, but Ms. Remcheck trusted them both, and they were just wandering around the City School's fourth floor. And there was Trevor's locker, wide open. Lee wanted to mess it up, but Joan was appalled by the idea.

When Lee reminded Joan that Trevor had recently called her "ironing board" in front of everyone during an assembly, a fierce light flared in her eyes. And then she proceeded to fold in half, with great precision, every piece of paper in Trevor's locker. And then she tore each piece of paper along that fold. It took forever, but they did it. And it was thrilling. Trevor, by the way, never said a word to anyone about it. Joan thought he was too embarrassed; Lee insisted Trevor simply hadn't noticed.

"But—" Lee said now, looking up at the lighthouse.

"I know," Joan said. "I know, we're not *supposed* to. But. We're *supposed* to be at California Dreaming. We're *supposed* to have families that can stay married. We're *supposed* to be going to the same high school. So, let's *suppose* ourselves into the lighthouse before we die."

Lee stared at the flimsy DO NOT ENTER sign. All they had to do was step over the chain.

Joan stepped over it and scurried up the metal stairs. She didn't wait for Lee, she just went, as if she heard Lee's mind change before it actually did. Things were like that between them. She knew he would join her, and sure enough, Lee stepped over the chain and followed.

They climbed onto the narrow platform that surrounded the main cabin and the enormous bell of the Fresnel lens. The tiny room, its iron half walls and high windows, seemed deliciously cozy from out here.

Joan turned the knob—it turned! The door swung in, and Lee and Joan piled into the tiny nine-sided room. Lee pulled the door shut, and they squirmed out of their backpacks and slid to the floor.

The tricky thing about fog, Lee knew, was that even though it blocked out the sun, the heat could still get through. On a freezing San Francisco day, the inside of a parked car could be an oven. It was the wind and wet that made you cold.

The high windows of the lighthouse made the room feel like a sauna. The heat enfolded them, and soon their brains thawed, Lee was the first to open his mouth, but Joan was the first to get her words out. She was quick like that; she could have been a gunslinger.

"You go," she said. "Tell me all about it. Tell me everything."

So Lee told her about the BLTs and the sudden announcement and the weird things the kitchen did, how he seemed to get stuck there. He didn't tell Joan he had seen her looking in the kitchen window. That was just too weird, and he wasn't quite sure if he'd actually seen her or just imagined her because he had wanted to see her.

"I was stuck in the kitchen for hours," he said, "then I was in bed and asleep. It was weird. I hated it. I hate it."

Leave it to Joan to ask the most obvious question of all, the one question Lee should have been asking, but couldn't get his brain to consider.

"Why?" she said. "Why are they getting a divorce? I don't get it. Donald and Barbara seem so, so . . .. so *not* unhappy. What did they tell you?"

Lee shuffled through the night before, kept trying to pull cards from that slippery deck. He heard his parents saying the things they had said but realized all their talk was meaningless. Parents: always talking but saying very little. He had no single idea *why* his parents were getting a divorce.

"I have no idea," he said. "In fact, it's totally stupid. They didn't give me one good reason. There are no good reasons. And I hate it."

Lee slammed his fist into the iron wall. Joan jumped, then offered up one of those sad, curvy, upside-down smiles of hers, the UNDERSTANDING.

"See," Joan said, "that's what I don't get. My parents, I get it. They're always yelling, always fighting. But your 'rents, I don't know. They're so calm."

Joan was right. His parents never argued. They did stuff together; everybody ate dinner together. They took vacations together, watched movies together, laughed together. Together. And now—not together. Crap.

Lee punched the wall again, though not as hard this time.

"I don't like it," he said. "I don't like it. I don't like it at all. I hate it."

Joan reached over, put her hand on his knee.

"Are you sure?" she said. "Are they going to do it for sure?"

Oh, yes, they were. It was hard to remember all the words his parents had used last night, but the tone was unmistakable. This was a decision that had been made. No do-overs.

Lee showed Joan the standard OH, YEAH.

"That's stupid," she said.

Lee wanted to say, right then, "This is *not* best for everyone," but he thought he might explode if he did. So he said something else. "Now you tell me."

It was clear to Lee that Joan remembered every single thing about last night with her parents. She started with the tapioca, replayed all the words, then told Lee how weird *her* dining room got, how she zoomed ahead of her parents into the future. Everything came pouring out of her.

"I don't want them to get divorced," she said. "I don't want to live in two stupid houses, with two different stupid bedrooms, and my two stupid parents."

"This sucks," Lee said.

"This totally sucks," Joan said.

"Sucks eggs."

The lighthouse got quieter than quiet's supposed to be. But Lee didn't need words to know what they were both thinking, and they were obviously thinking the same things. This field trip sucked, high school was going to suck, and divorce sucked most of all.

"What are we gonna do?" Joan asked.

"Eat?" Lee said.

They shared the tried and true WHY DIDN'T WE THINK OF THIS EARLIER?

Lee had two barbecued-pork buns and gave one to Joan; Joan cut her super-chicken burrito in half with a plastic knife. Lee had strawberries, Joan grapes. Ginger ale and root beer; thin mints and madeleines.

They ate it all up. And they talked. But they kept circling back to the same idea. It all sucked. EVERYTHING.

"What are we gonna do?" Joan asked.

"I'll build a time machine, then we can go back in time and fix everything—including this field trip—and then life will be perfect. That's how you do it in movies."

And Lee could almost see it, going back in time, doing one little thing that would make his parents happy again.

"Or," Joan said, "we could just leap into the future, way far ahead, and skip everything in between."

Joan snapped the last of the thin mints in two and gave Lee the bigger half.

EXCELLENT.

They nibbled quietly, stretching out the moment, trying to keep the moment right where it was.

Lee rested his head against the wall, closed his eyes, and the foggy warmth wrapped him up.

He was walking down an unknown street, and just as he got to the corner, he misjudged the step, and his foot jerked off the curb.

He snapped awake for the briefest moment, but instantly fell back to sleep, lulled by the bright yellow sunshine that beamed into the lighthouse.

FOUR

The Big Nap – A Dose of Clarity – A National Landmark Goes Missing – The Mysterious Stranger – Forward, March!

Just before Joan woke up in the toasty lighthouse, she was visited by a strange dream.

She was walking down endless narrow alleys, dark twisting alleys, and she had no idea where she was. The hardest part of the dream was staying on the wooden walkway that swayed beneath her. If she fell, she knew she'd fall in the mud, and this thought terrified her.

"This dream is all wrong," she said out loud in her dream, and wondered if she had said it out loud in the real world. At that moment, her foot slipped off the walkway, but she snapped awake before she landed in the mud.

Joan knew where she was—she and Lee were in the Fort Point lighthouse on the worst field trip ever in the entire history of bad field trips and on the worst day ever in the history of, well, history.

The fog that had shrouded San Francisco all morning was gone, the sun blazing. The lighthouse was no longer toasty, more like pizza-oven hot.

Lee stood with his back to Joan, staring out the lighthouse windows. Even though she could not see his face, Joan knew he was smiling. Lee often smiled with his whole body.

Joan sat up.

"You've gotta check this out," Lee said without turning around. "It's beautiful."

Joan pulled herself up and joined him at the windows. They were looking east, towards the city. The sun was knife sharp, the bay sparkled blue-green, and the hills were golden.

It *was* beautiful, Joan saw. But very wrong.

There was no city where there should be a city. Where there definitely had been a city that morning. Instead, in the distance, only a scattering of squat buildings, and plumes of black smoke rising into the sky. No skyscrapers, no traffic-jammed streets. No city.

Her first thought was *earthquake*. There had been a huge earthquake, and San Francisco had burned to the ground, but she and Lee had fallen asleep and missed all the commotion.

Or maybe she was still asleep.

No. She was awake and she knew it. She didn't need to pinch herself. The goose bumps she felt, the air in her lungs, the solid floor under her feet, all told her she was awake and the world was real. The sky above her seemed more than real.

"Have you ever seen anything like it?" Lee said.

"Look up," Joan said.

She pulled him to the ocean side of the lighthouse and pointed to the sky.

"I know," he said. "It's awesome."

"It's gone," she said.

"Gone?"

"The bridge," she said in a whisper. "The Golden Gate Bridge is gone."

She was almost crying, almost shaking, just about ready to scream.

"Ho. Ly. Cow," Lee said, and that about summed it up.

The Golden Gate Bridge was not where it was supposed to be. And no earthquake had pulled it down. There was no rubble in the water where the bridge had once stood; there was simply no bridge.

Lee and Joan did the only thing they could possibly do: They stared. No thinking, just staring.

A loud pop and rumble shook the lighthouse's tower. The noise came from behind them, and they rushed to it. A small white cloud hung above one of the cannons on the barbette tier.

Cannons? Joan asked herself. There were no cannons on the top of the fort. Any field tripper knew that. All the cannons were in the main courtyard, plugged with concrete. Fact.

Three soldiers were busy reloading the cannon, their uniforms pale blue against the bright green grass.

Grass? There was no grass on the barbette tier; it was all asphalt. Joan knew this for another fact.

How weird that she should be taking notice of the grass. Shouldn't she be more concerned about the soldiers?

The soldiers were trying, it seemed, to reload one of their cannons. One of them, short and loud, was obviously in charge. He yelled at two taller and scruffy soldiers, barking and barking. There was a lot of barking and a lot of running around, but the cannon didn't seem to be getting much loaded. These were not rangers or docents dressed in period costume; they were too dirty, too miserable looking, too loud.

These soldiers were playing for real. That cannon was real.

Lee grabbed Joan's elbow and pulled her down, which seemed like a pretty good idea.

They stared at each other and, lickety-split, invented a whole new LOOK. NONONONONONONONO.

"Lee," Joan said. She felt a tremor in her voice. "Uh, can you please tell me where we are?"

"I'm not sure," he said—his voice was shaking a bit, too—"if that's the right question."

Please, Joan prayed, please don't say that the right question is not "*Where* are we?" but "*When* are we?"

"I think," he said, "the question is 'WHEN are we?'"

"Don't say that," she hissed at him. But he was right. *When* the bleep were they?

This was an impossible idea, but it had to be true. And so Joan pinched herself, hard, just in case. Yep, that hurt. Pretty real.

Joan opened her mouth to speak, but whatever lame sentence she was conjuring died when she heard the clanging footfalls on the lighthouse stairs.

Joan froze and turned to Lee for help. Unfortunately, Lee had turned to Joan for help. Who was going to help whom?

And then the door of the lighthouse flew open, but instead of a soldier training a rifle on them, there stood in the doorway a man dressed all in black. When the stranger saw Joan and Lee, he looked as surprised as Joan felt.

The stranger wore a black suit that could only be described as old-fashioned. The tails of his coat were long, and from his black vest, the silver chain of a pocket watch gleamed. His black shoes were pointy and worn. His reddish brown hair was puffy under a lumpy black hat, his mustache reddish and puffy, too. He was older than Joan's brothers, but much younger than her parents.

Joan wanted to look at Lee, and she could feel Lee wanting to look at her, but there was this mysterious stranger to look at. And the stranger was looking at them. Everyone was just staring, taking it all in. Joan knew the three of them shared the same LOOK. YOU CAN'T BE SERIOUS.

A nervous smile broke out under the man's mustache. He swiped the hat off his head and slapped his knee with it.

"Well, dog my cats," the stranger said. "I sure as heck didn't expect to find you two. Boy howdy."

Joan scrunched down and scooted right on up against Lee. All her weird feelings were coming into a single focus—panic.

"Who are you?" she screamed. "Get away from us.

Go away. You have to go away now." All those years of "stranger danger" lectures were finally paying off.

The stranger looked back toward the cannon, then dropped to a crouch, out of sight of the window. He put a finger to his lips and opened his eyes wide.

Lee put a hand on Joan's arm and squeezed real tight. He knew how to keep things calm; he was good at that. They looked at each other. BREATHE.

"Who are you?" Lee whispered.

The stranger put up his hands, palms out. Joan knew this LOOK, the JUST A SECOND. He reached into his coat pocket and pulled out . . . Was it a gun? Was it a knife? Was it a? . . . The stranger pulled out a ratty old piece of string and wound it three times around a lock of his reddish hair. He was muttering to himself. Then the stranger got on his knees and turned around three times, like a dog trying to find the right spot to lie down. The stranger sat down, legs crossed, smiling nervously again.

"Not from round these parts, are you?" the stranger said.

He had a Southern accent, like that new kid at school, Dale, the one from North Carolina. It was a gentle voice, the stranger's.

Hold it right there. Joan was not going to let herself be tricked by some cool accent. Practically the same thing as taking candy.

Joan turned to Lee. Why wasn't he saying anything? "Lee."

Lee turned, but he just looked at her with that big goofy grin of his.

"Listen, I know you're afraid," the stranger said. "As you ought to be. I was quaking in my boots the first time I came unstuck. I will do my best to explain everything to you, but here and now is not the time and place."

"'Unstuck'?" Lee said. There was no scream in his voice, just a bit of "Ooh, how cool."

"Unstuck in time," the stranger said. "My friend Kurt taught me that one. Good description, unstuck in time."

"'Unstuck in time'?" Lee said, but Joan shushed him.

The stranger unwound the string from his hair, put it in his pocket.

"I mean you no harm," he said. "I'm a friend and, for now, the only one you have. Hear me. Do you know what year this is?"

"Impossible," Joan said. "Time travel is impossible, and that's a fact."

Joan looked at Lee again, but he was still smiling his "Ooh, how cool" smile.

"Impossible," was all Joan could say.

"One would like to think so," the stranger said. "But follow this trail. The two of you, in whatever *when* you are from, you fell asleep in this lighthouse, didn't you? And when you woke, everything was changed."

GULP.

"How'd you know that?" Lee asked.

"Because it happened to me, right here in this very same lighthouse. And it's why I've come back. I was hoping to come unstuck again. But you two have altered my plans."

"We're from 2012," Lee said.

"Lord a-mercy," the stranger said. "That is one long stretch of river. No wonder you're all a little leery. Let me extend a hospitable welcome to 1864."

"1864?!" Lee could not help himself.

Joan, however, was not going to suffer this nonsense.

"Impossible," she said.

"Better get used to it," the stranger said. "Sooner's better than later. I put it to you, young lady, was it 2012 when you woke up this morning?"

It *had* been 2012. But Joan wasn't going to admit it.

"Now," the stranger said, "you just peek out that window and try to convince yourself it's still 2012."

Joan didn't need to peek out the window. She merely had to look up and see that the Golden Gate Bridge was no longer there, or not there *yet,* or whatever—but clearly not where it was supposed to be.

"Fine," she said. "Let's say I buy that, let's say it is 1864. Fine. Why should we trust *you?*"

The stranger started to speak, but Lee interrupted, drawing Joan towards him with his voice.

"Because he *knows,*" Lee said. "And you know and I know, too, that something totally freaky is going on. So, if he knows—"

The cannon boomed again; Joan's ears emptied out a bit. She saw the white cloud of the cannon's explosion rise past the lighthouse window. The stranger checked his watch.

"Best get a move on," he said. "The troops'll muster in about a minute or so, and we don't want to be caught here."

Lee started to rise, but Joan pushed him back down.

"No," she said. "It may be 1864 or whatever, but why would we trust a total stranger? If we are *unstuck*"—she said the word with a whine attached to it—"and this lighthouse is some crazy time machine, as you say, then we're staying here until we get back home."

"Joan!" Lee said, but she silenced him with a very stern DON'T EVEN.

A bugle sounded from the courtyard, followed by shouting and footsteps.

"They're mustering," the stranger said. "I suggest you be quick as a hare with your decision. It is 1864, there's a war on, and soldiers don't look kindly on strangers in their midst."

The bugle rang again.

"Quick now," the stranger said. "I have the proper papers to be here, but not papers for you two. I am happy to help my fellow travelers, but I will not hang on your behalf. You may come with me, or you may explain to the business end of a rifle how it is you come from the future."

The stranger was getting up, ready to move.

"We'll just tell them we got lost," Joan said. "We won't even mention the future."

Together, all three of them looked at Joan and Lee's feet. Joan's Kixes were silver with neon green stripes, Lee's Kixes blue with neon orange stripes. Not the height of fashion in 1864. And their backpacks, Joan's Creepazoids T-shirt, her cell phone?

YOIKS.

"Fine," Joan said. "Where are we going?"

"Away from here," the stranger said.

"How do we get out?" she said.

"Cunning."

The bugle again, a long, drawn-out refrain.

"Let's go," Lee said. "By the way, I'm Lee and this is Joan."

"Sam," the stranger said. "Sam Clemens. My pleasure.

Now, follow me. And let's be Indian about it. Low and swift and silent."

Sam eased open the door and backed out of the lighthouse. Joan and Lee grabbed their backpacks; Joan urged Lee ahead of her.

They crouched, tiptoeing along the barbette tier towards the granite staircase.

Joan felt like a spy, a fugitive. Maybe this wasn't a dream after all. Maybe this was a movie they'd fallen into. That could happen, right? Made as much sense as falling into 1864.

Sam led them down to the second floor, and from there they sidled into what Joan knew were the soldiers' barracks. A long series of open doorways led down the length of the fort, each door, from this perspective, smaller than the last. Sam pulled them into the first barracks' room, wall-to-wall bunk beds. At the foot of each bunk, a large wooden chest.

What were they doing in here? Joan felt more trapped than escaping.

"What are we? . . ." she started to whisper.

"Now, Joan," Sam whispered back, "I will, I promise, oblige you any answers I can find. But let's wait until we are outside a fortress teeming with armed soldiers who are just bored enough to shoot the first stranger they see."

"But—"

Lee put his hand on her arm and offered up a LOOK Joan had seen from him a thousand times. CHILL.

"Find yourself a uniform," Sam said. "The best way to escape a place you are not wanted is to look as if you belong there."

Sam was opening trunks, pulling out caps and jackets and pants. Lee did the same.

"Here," Sam said, and he thrust a pile of blue uniform into Joan's arms. "Put these on."

"I will not undress in front—"

"Over your own clothes," Sam said. "Make you look bigger, more soldiery."

Joan and Lee pulled on pants with dark blue stripes down each leg, then short, brass-buttoned jackets. The material was stiff, heavy, and didn't smell all that good. But the uniforms fit surprisingly well.

After slipping on his pants, Sam shook off his black coat and put on a soldier's. The coat had three yellow stripes on each sleeve. Sam tore off his hat and put on a blue cap with a shiny black bill. He handed a soldier's short-billed cap to Lee, then turned to Joan and gestured around his head. She pulled a scrunchy from her wrist, made a ponytail and folded it on top of her head. She pulled the cap down, but Sam pulled it down far over her eyes.

"You especially," Sam said to Joan, "keep your face hid."

"Why me?"

"Uh, you're a girl?" Lee said.

Sam and Lee stuffed Sam's coat and their backpacks into the soldiers' backpacks. Each one had a bedroll attached to it.

Outside the bugle called again. Loud men were shouting.

"Well, troops, atten-hut!" Sam whispered. "Follow my lead. Show me what fine thespians you are."

"Thespians?" Lee asked.

"Actors," Joan whispered.

"Forward, march!" Sam bellowed.

As they marched out of the barracks, Joan bringing up the rear, she looked down the tunnel of doorways, and there, at the far end, she saw another man dressed all in black. The man was looking right at her. He was moving towards them. Waving? A little "eep" escaped Joan, and she reached out to alert Lee, but before her hand got to his elbow, this man in black faded away, like a thin fog shot through with sun. Gone.

Okay, even weirder. But Joan decided to say nothing about this other man in black. Things were weird enough already. Besides, she thought if she did say something about him, she'd have to consider how he'd disappeared, just like that, and then the scream might return to her voice.

The bugle rang out again, bright and furious, and the courtyard below erupted with action, the prim ranks of soldiers breaking into seeming chaos.

Sam led them to the spiral staircase again, and down they went, hugging the interior wall, while soldiers streamed up past them. In the courtyard, Sam led them through packs of soldiers all busy at being soldiers. None of the real soldiers paid the slightest mind to the three new recruits.

When they turned into the sallyport tunnel, Joan saw at the far end the bright spot of daylight that led outside. But between here and freedom stood two armed guards, each holding a long rifle, each rifle mounted with a nasty bayonet.

"Halt," one of the guards called. "Who goes there?"

"Sergeant Leghorn," Sam called. "And his two charges."

Sam marched right up to the soldier. This soldier was only a teenager, really, not much older than Joan.

"State your business," the soldier said. He was trying to look very serious.

"Well, now, boy," Sam said. "I say, I say, I like the cut of your jib. That's some fine soldiering there. Now, since you asked in such a proper manner, I will oblige you.

Why, we're on a reconnaissance sortie, don't you know? Colonel's orders." Sam's voice was different now, deep and loud, and kind of ugly.

The soldier stretched up and looked over Sam's shoulder, then he looked Lee and Joan up and down. Joan felt the second soldier close behind her.

The first soldier took a step back from Sam and aimed the bayonet at Sam's heart.

"Sergeant, sir," he said. "With all due respect. Inform the guards on duty just what in the name of our good God are those two wearing on their feet. Ain't no regulation boots I've ever heard of."

Everyone looked at Lee and Joan's feet. Their Kixes.

"Wouldn't you know, son," Sam said to the soldier. "I'd heard tell you was about the best guard that ever done guarded a sallyport ever. And Jehosaphat, was they right. You have passed your test with flying colors. These here *shoes*, they are a matter of utmost secrecy, hence our sneaking out during drill. These here shoes, why, they might just win the war."

Both soldiers looked rather stupidly at Sam. Joan almost laughed.

"Can you two privates keep a secret real private? Only the toppest of the brass knows about this."

The soldiers nodded vigorously. Everyone loved a secret.

Sam pushed the bayonet to one side, as if it were a spider web he did not wish to break.

"See, I says, see," Sam bragged on, "agents of the French government have offered these new shoes to Mr. Lincoln. They are, as the French say, I say, *hors de combat*, that is, out of combat. Savvy?"

The soldiers nodded, furiously this time.

"My charges here are to field test them on this fine day. I only trust you with this intelligence because of the fine things said about the both of you. That's right, the both of you. It is apparent to all that you will not be privates much longer, not with such inborn acuity. Now, remember, you haven't seen a thing, now have you?"

The two soldiers stepped back, snapped to attention, lowered their rifles to their sides. They wore grins worthy of Lee.

"Sir, yes, sir," the first soldier bellowed. "Carry on, sir."

Sam saluted and marched them out of the dark sallyport tunnel into the brilliant sunshine. Joan turned around.

The two soldiers stood in front of the sallyport entrance now, their goofy smiles all ablaze. Joan laughed a little at the two soldiers. Some people will believe anything, she thought.

FIVE

A Dinosaur Would Be Better – Backtrack Trick – Rebel Spies – Lee Makes a Fine Idiot – Boy or Girl

Of course, Lee thought, of course, my house isn't here. Nobody's is.

He and Joan and the stranger who called himself Sam stood at the top of a steep cliff that looked out over a San Francisco that was both totally familiar and totally alien to Lee. His house should be right over there, just past where Golden Gate Park should be. But his house wasn't there and neither was the park. Lee's stomach dropped right out from under him. The soldier's uniform he wore was suddenly hot and scratchy.

Until this second, Lee found time travel a pretty interesting adventure. Joan had been freaked out by it all, he knew. More than freaked out. She was used to thinking things through, insisting on finding the logic in the world. In the lighthouse, Lee had heard in her screamy voice that she simply didn't want to believe they'd been transported to 1864, or whenever they were. And she was hankering to argue with, what seemed to Lee, an obvious fact—they were no longer in 2012.

But from the moment Lee looked out the lighthouse windows and saw the city that was no longer there, he'd been stoked about the whole time-travel thing. How could you not love it? Sam and the cannons and dressing up and fooling the guards—it was a hoot! This might actually turn out to be the best field trip anyone anywhere ever went on. Maybe even better than California Dreaming.

When they left the fort, Sam marched them along the bay towards Crissy Field. But there was no Crissy Field, only, well, field, and some marshland, and a whole lot of birds. Then they turned south, into the Presidio, only this was no Presidio Lee ever knew. It was all dune grass and sand and bare hills, a few patches of beach strawberry. There was no freeway that cut through here, no forest of pine and eucalyptus, no enormous Army cemetery. There were no white and pink houses covering the city's hillsides, no nothing that Lee knew should be there.

But still, it was a San Francisco he recognized. There was Alcatraz Island out in the bay and, far across the bay, Mount Diablo. Totally familiar; totally alien. And kind of awesomely cool.

Then they reached the top of a rocky ridge near where Pacific Heights normally was. The three of them stood together silently. There was no Pacific Heights and, beyond that, no Richmond District, no Sunset District, no May Lee's Free Chinese Delivery, no Irving Variety, no Tutti-Frutti Toys for All Ages. Only grass-covered hills and a few scattered farmhouses. There was certainly no Lee's house and, of course, no Lee's parents.

Foolishly Lee had counted on his house being there. But you couldn't travel back in time 148 years—he did the math—and expect a house built in 1908 to be there. That wouldn't make any sense.

The big stomach drop again. He and Joan were more than a hundred years from home. That morning Lee hadn't really cared if he ever saw his parents again; they were being so ridiculous with all their divorce talk. But now, he thought it might be nice to at least talk to them, see how they were doing. He wondered if they even knew he was gone yet. What time was it in the future?

"Right over there," Joan was saying. Sam looked to where she pointed. "My house is usually right over there."

Joan's house was gone, too. Lee hadn't been looking for that curveball.

"Sam," Lee said, "I think I'd very much like to go home now."

Sam turned to Lee. For some reason, Lee trusted him. Maybe it was the fact that Sam hadn't turned them over to the soldiers, or that he wasn't freaked out by the whole time-travel thing, or maybe that there wasn't really any choice but to trust him, given how untrustworthy the rest of reality had become lately. So when Lee saw the worried tilt of Sam's soldier's cap, his stomach dropped again.

"That's what we all want," Sam said. "And we're going to do our best to make that happen. But Lee, I suggest you first take a deep breath. You look a little green about the gills."

The instant Sam said, "green about the gills," Lee felt his knees buckle, and he thought he might actually collapse and might just go ahead and barf while he was collapsing. He took the biggest, loudest breath he could. "Breathe, stupid, breathe," his brain was saying.

"Okay," he said. "I'm okay."

Joan was suddenly in front of him, smiling, and Lee could almost pretend to relax. Joan was definitely less freaked out now, and if that were true, Lee might get back there himself one day. He found a little smile he could afford to spend.

"Good," Joan said.

Sam pushed back the black bill of his soldier's cap, and Lee could see his whole face now.

"I know this is all quite confusing," Sam said. "But the clearer our heads, the better for us all. And the sooner you'll get home."

Get home? Lee liked that idea, and he especially liked the idea that Sam had said it. Lee made the "ai-ee-ee-ai-ee-ai," sound that cartoon characters make after they've been hit on the head. "Ai-ee-ee-ai-ee-ai."

Sam tried to make the same sound and did a pretty good job of it, too. Lee found a slightly bigger smile he'd forgotten he had. But no sooner had Lee pasted on that smile, when a bugle call sounded behind them.

The three of them stood as still as possible, their heads cocked, like dogs listening for the unhearable.

Lee felt the pounding of the horses' hooves before he actually heard it. Soldiers on horseback, cavalry.

What Lee thought he could really use right about now was a dinosaur—a T. rex, maybe a triceratops, heck, even a boring old apatosaurus. In time-travel movies, there was always a dinosaur. When your time machine landed, some dinosaur was always chasing you. Then, after some more dinosaur chases, you fixed your time machine, set the dial for home, and everything turned out all right.

A dinosaur, Lee imagined, had to be worlds better than soldiers and horses and guns and bayonets. You might outsmart a dinosaur, but you couldn't outrun a bullet.

"I thought we'd fooled them," Joan said.

"Even the biggest dullards," Sam said, "eventually figure out they've been fooled. And then they get angry."

"Look," Joan whispered. Lee obediently looked.

Up the hillside they'd come was a wide swath of tamped-down grass, a clear map to where they stood. They might as well have left a trail of bread crumbs— huge neon bread crumbs.

"We'll have to backtrack," Sam said. "Throw them off the scent. Watch me."

Sam broke for an outcropping of rock several yards away. When he got there, he twisted around, then motioned in the other direction, where the rocky ridge continued. Lee was still concentrating on breathing; luckily, Joan was paying attention and in charge of everything. She pulled Lee along to the far rocks. The grass path forked now, a perfect *T*. It looked as if the party had split up, the two trails disappearing on the rocks.

Sam commenced to walking backwards now, with high, exaggerated steps. Lee and Joan walked backwards, too, retracing their own steps, making sure that the tall grass stayed bent in the proper direction.

The soldiers were drawing nearer; along with the hoofbeats came the sound of crackling brush.

Sam's backtrack was a nifty trick, but now what? Lee was hoping that Joan was still on top of it all.

Sam leaped a little to one side and scrambled down the steep cliff face. Oh, now Lee got it. He and Joan leaped out of their tracks and followed Sam, scraping over some very pointy and unforgiving rocks.

They came to rest halfway down the cliff, hidden under the canopy of a three-trunked manzanita that grew from a narrow ledge. They stood with their backs against the cliff face.

Above them, the hoofbeats arrived at the top of the cliff. There was a great clattering, and some loose rocks rained through the manzanita's branches. A cloud of dust arose from the top of the cliff and floated out over the valley. Lee peered up, where he saw the nodding head of one of the horses, its ginormous nostrils flaring. He could hear the expelled breath of the horse, could almost smell that grassy smell. And was that the glint of a bayonet?

A long silence filled the day.

"Tarnation," a frustrated voice bellowed. "C Troop, circle around to the west, towards Cliff House. F Troop, with me to the east. We'll circle them in. Send word to the battery; lock down all the ports. Those rebel spies will not escape Colonel Michael T. Reinhart. Now, h'yah."

There was a single snap of leather against horse, and the commotion of the troops rose up again, dividing, fading into the east and the west.

Lee's strength had never been processing tons of information at once. He was "considered," that's what his mom said. It was Joan's job to excel at fast thinking. But to be fair, a good deal had happened in the last little while, so it's not an insult to say it took Lee some time to add up what he was just now adding up. If this was 1864, then the war Sam had mentioned was the Civil War, and therefore, he and Sam and Joan might well be seen as rebel spies. That could not be good. A dinosaur would be better in many ways.

"Wha—" Joan started to say, but Sam put up his hand. They all waited long seconds. Silence.

"If I may be so bold"—Sam spoke now—"might I suggest we beat it out of here. I know Colonel Michael T. Reinhart, and he will not rest until he finds those spies."

"Where?" Joan asked.

Lee really didn't care where, just not here.

"Yonder," Sam said. "San Francisco proper. Once we get there, we'll be safe. Hard to find a man in any city, but San Francisco more than most. Good place to disappear."

There was the city. Lee had been so busy looking at what was not in this San Francisco that he'd forgotten to look at what was there. Two ridges of hills to the east stood a wooden tower of some kind and, beyond, streets and houses, thickening with every block, a much better place to hide than this cliff.

Lee was ready to go, but Joan, of course, had a question. "Where in the city?"

"My humble abode," Sam said. "We'll be safe there until we figure out how to get you two stuck in your own time again."

Joan peeled herself from the cliff and turned to Sam. "You don't know, do you?" she said. "I mean, how we get back."

"Not yet," Sam said, and he smiled, and Lee tried very hard to be comforted by that smile. "But I'd also like to suggest that we're better off figuring it out together and not while we're facing a firing squad."

Joan turned to Lee now, who was slowly peeling himself away from the cliff. They exchanged possibly the most complex LOOK they'd ever exchanged. What to call it? With this one LOOK, they asked each other countless questions: Do you trust Sam? Do you think this is the right decision? Are we still in this together? Can this really be happening? And the answer to all these questions was the same: yes. Joan and Lee didn't have to say anything, didn't have to nod, or even raise an eyebrow. They were agreed; they would trust Sam. For now.

Joan had one last question, though. "How do we get all the way over there without being seen?"

Another good question, Joan, Lee thought. The countryside in this San Francisco was practically bare.

Sam pointed to a farmhouse not far away.

"I suggest we change our clothes again," he said. "They're looking for us, that is, what they think are three men, so we should definitely not be us. We're going to need some new duds."

In the backyard of the farmhouse lines of laundry hung still in the bright sunshine.

"Sam," Joan said, "that's stealing. That is so not right."

"That is true," Sam said, "if you look at it one way. If we were to run up and steal those clothes, why, yes, that would be stealing. But if we were to conjure a worthy scheme and call that scheme an adventure, why, you might say we'd earned those clothes."

"I'm all for adventure," Lee managed to squeak out. "As long as it gets us out of here."

Sam and Lee both turned to Joan. As if to remind them where they were, a bugle sang out over the valley.

"Adventure it is," Joan said.

They crept down the cliff to the base, and Sam led them from there into a tree-cloaked gulley, through which a parched creek twisted. It was great to be in the shade again. The day was weird hot, and his uniform was so heavy, Lee was sweating like a pig.

"Sam," Lee called past Joan. "What day is it today?"

"September the sixth."

Well, Lee thought, that explains the heat. It was Indian summer now in San Francisco, when the skies were always bright and sharp, the temperatures scorching. Weird, Lee thought, to have changed seasons, too, though he couldn't explain why that should be any weirder than changing centuries.

They trotted along until they came even with the farmhouse. Sam threw himself on the creek's bank and peered out through an opening in the low-hanging trees. Lee and Joan came up behind him. Not fifty yards away, a plain, boxy wooden house sat and, beyond the house, an open-sided barn and acres of fenced-in rolling hills dotted with black-and-white and brown cows.

"Now what?" This was both Joan and Lee.

"Pay heed," Sam said, and he sketched out an elaborate plan that was part playacting, part espionage, part athletics.

"Well, okay," Joan said. "I guess that's better than just stealing flat out."

First, they all snaked out of their soldiers' uniforms and stuffed them into two of the packs, then hid those under a prickly bush. Lee turned his *Meet The Fuddles* T-shirt inside out, so the picture couldn't be seen. Lee and Joan's jeans, Sam pointed out to them, would not cause any confusion. Their jeans looked just like the jeans half of San Francisco wore in 1864.

But Lee's blue-and-orange Kixes were a problem, and anyway, Sam said, "no self-respectin' boy would be caught dead in shoes on such a gorgeous not-going-to-church day," so Lee took them off. Joan kept hers on; she would need to run fast.

Then Sam and Joan proceeded to kick dust all over Lee, from head to toe. Lee even rubbed dirt on his face; Joan mussed up his hair for him. He looked perfectly idiotic, and that was perfect for their plan.

Lee climbed up out of the creek bed and made his way to the dirt road that led to the farmhouse. He walked in a crazy, jerky way, muttering to himself. He walked through the little wooden gate and up to the front door and started pounding on it. Sure enough, the door flew open.

The woman at the door was right out of a Western movie: a faded cornflower dress, her graying hair pulled back tight, her creased face all frowns.

"Young man?" she asked, "are you all right?"

Lee did what he was supposed to do—he acted like an idiot, one of those old-timey village idiots. He made noises but did not speak, he rolled his eyes in the back of his head, he jerked and swayed, he drooled, and once fell down. But he kept trying to communicate, dropping a real word here and there. It was his job to occupy the farm wife for as long as possible. She kept asking him questions and frowning concerned frowns, and Lee just kept acting like an idiot. He was pretty good at it, if he said so himself.

Meanwhile, Lee saw Joan and Sam rise up out of the creek bed and spring across the back lot, disappearing behind the farmhouse. Moments later, they went running back again, Sam carrying a loose bundle of clothes. They folded back into the tree line of the creek.

And just in time. The farmwife had run out of patience.

"You poor critter," she said, searching through a drawstring purse attached to her waist. "I don't know if this will help you, or if you are merely a rapscallion, but

Lord, I don't have time for this. I've a world of chores."
She pulled a coin from her purse and handed it to Lee.
"Lord have mercy on you," she said, and closed the
door.

A penny? A lousy penny? Lee thought he'd acted the
idiot much more than a penny's worth. But this was
1864 money. Maybe he was rich.

He jerked and stumbled out the gate and back down
the road a piece, then sprinted low across the open grass-
land to Sam and Joan. When Lee found them, Sam had
spread out the bundle of clothes they'd "adventured"
from the farmhouse, and he and Joan were sizing up
their disguise possibilities.

Sam slathered mud on one of the packs, to camou-
flage its Army blue, then stuffed the 2012 backpacks and
his own coat into it.

From the booty on the ground, Sam picked up a long
black shirt and slipped it on. The shirt fell to his shoes,
more like a long dress. Then he tied his hair back with
that ratty old piece of string of his and put on a cone-
shaped straw hat, which he wore low over his face. He
looked almost invisible to Lee.

What was left was a wool jacket and a bell-shaped
dress and short-brimmed bonnet. Oh, this would work
fine: Lee as a boy, Joan as a girl.

"And I shall be," Sam said, "your Chinese manservant. I'll be able to hang behind you, as all servants must, and from there, keep my eye on anyone we might meet, look out for trouble. Now, Joan . . ."

Sam picked up the bonnet and put it on Joan's head. It looked nice, Lee thought—she looked pretty. But Sam shook his head.

"That simply won't do," he said.

Instead of putting her into the dress, Sam had Joan step out of her shoes and keep her jeans on. Over her *Creepozoids* T-shirt, Sam buttoned up the short brown jacket. She made a pretty good boy.

But if she was the boy . . .

Sam held up the white, bell-shaped dress with pink roses on it. He handed it to Lee.

"This ought to be a fit," Sam said.

Uh, no, you seem to have made a huge error, see, that's a dress, and I'm a boy. This was what Lee was thinking. What Lee said was, "No way."

"You must," Sam said. He picked up the bonnet and plopped it on Lee's head. "Perfect."

"Why me?" Lee said. "I don't want to."

"Because it's all we have, and besides, a girl is perfect for our ruse," Sam said, "that's why."

"But she's a girl."

Lee did not understand what was happening. Time travel was one thing, but dressing up as a girl?

"C'mon, Lee, put it on," Joan said. She was trying very hard, Lee saw, not to laugh out loud.

"But—"

Fine, Lee thought, I'll be the girl, though I don't understand it at all.

He slipped the dress over his head; it covered his Kixes.

"Just look at you," Sam said. "My, my."

"Ravishing," Joan said.

Enough already. This was the exact opposite of both fair and fun.

"No," Lee said. "I don't see why I have to be the girl, that's crazy. Give me one good reason why."

"Because," Sam said. He put his black slouch hat on Joan and pulled it far down over her face. "Because that bonnet doesn't cover her face, and this hat does. She needs to keep her face covered, not you."

"But why?"

Both Lee and Joan turned seriously to Sam. There was something dark in the words he spoke. He looked hard at Joan.

"You are Chinese, correct?" Sam said.

Joan nodded.

"If anyone finds you with us," Sam said, "we'll all wish we'd been captured by those soldiers instead." He took Joan by the shoulders. "Keep your head down, your face hidden. San Francisco is a dangerous place. Especially for you."

SIX

A Pinkie Swear Is Sacred – The Chinese Menace – An Up and Down City – Fancy New Duds – Fine Upstanding Citizens

Before Joan had the chance to blurt, "Hold on there, bucko," Sam was moving along the creek bed. A couple of sharp bends on, and he flew up the bank.

It didn't seem quite right to Joan that after the words "Chinese" and "danger" were uttered so closely together that Sam would want to leave the safety of the creek bed. Joan had only just accepted the fact that this was 1864 not 2012, and now Sam's scary words—too much. But she wasn't about to argue the point. She followed close on Sam's heels, dying to ask questions but dying more to keep up with him. Lee followed, too, though slowly. The dress he wore made climbing less than graceful.

They emerged where the dirt road from the farmhouse brushed the creek, and Sam stopped there, waiting for Lee.

Joan went right up to Sam and stared hard until he finally looked up at her from under his straw hat.

"Okay," she barked. "What exactly do you mean by 'Chinese' and 'danger'? I demand to know right now."

Joan's principles had kicked in again. She was not going to move one single inch until her question was answered.

"Keep moving, Joan," Sam said. "You and Lee walk ahead of me. I must stay several steps behind you all the while."

"No," she said. And she actually crossed her arms and stomped her foot.

Lee put his hand on her shoulder with a very soft, "C'mon."

Joan didn't turn from Sam, didn't take her eyes away from him, but made it clear she was talking to Lee when she spoke. "Look, last time I checked, I was the only real Chinese person here, so if you don't mind, I'd like Sam to answer one simple question."

Lee made no noise at all.

"Here is a first answer," Sam said. "I am now your

Chinese servant, and as such, you must not talk to me. Unless you're going to yell at me. You must walk far ahead of me, pretend I do not exist. That is how the fine upstanding citizens of San Francisco in 1864, at least, treat their Chinese neighbors. We cannot afford undue suspicion. Now walk."

Those darn principles of hers. Joan was not going to budge.

"You keep saying you're going to tell us everything," she said, still staring hard at Sam. "But I want to know now."

"If you'll proceed, I'll tell you what I can, I swear on it."

Joan wanted to believe Sam; he *seemed* trustworthy. But so many untrustworthy things had happened today.

There was only one surefire method, one absolutely sacred way to gauge a person's trustworthiness. Joan would extend this offer to Sam, and if he understood, she would wait to hear what she needed to hear. She would trust him.

"Pinkie swear?" Joan said more than asked, a challenge more than a question. She lifted her right hand, her pinkie extended.

"Pinkie swear," Sam said with no hesitation. He nodded gravely. He hooked his pinkie with Joan's.

"Pinkie swear," Lee said, all at once, next to them.

Lee joined his pinkie with theirs, then the three repeated the magic phrase—"pinkie swear"—and in unison, they raised their hands, then brought them down together, the pinkie-swear shake. Sam not only knew about the pinkie swear, it seemed he knew its etiquette. Not once did his eyes turn away from Joan or Lee. Sam was serious.

Joan couldn't help but wonder—given this was 1864—how many centuries people had been exchanging this sacred bond. Maybe the pinkie swear was the glue that held civilization together. Immediately, she calmed down.

"Shall we?" Sam said, and they set off towards the city, Sam trailing.

"Now," he said, from three paces behind them, "I don't know about your San Francisco, but you'll find this one an often brutal place. Why, it's little more than a frontier town, barely fifteen years old. You'll still find Indians living nearby and, occasionally, a bear or mountain lion will wander through. And those are the safest of the critters you'll meet. The ones you want to keep an eye on are the newly arrived, those other critters who've come here to find their fortunes since the Gold Rush of '49. These are an ornery and unpredictable lot."

"Sam," Joan snapped. "Chinese? Danger?"

"Joan," Lee snapped rather snappishly. "The pinkie swear?"

"Indeed," Sam said. "I do tend to mosey into a story. My apologies. Ahem. Along with those who came from the east to find their fortunes in San Francisco, many came from the west, too, mainly from China. East or west, no matter, no one found much fortune here, neither the pot of gold nor the gold mountain. But they stayed. And to make up for their losses—and their embarrassment—they like to blame other people for their own foolishness."

Joan recognized the words "gold mountain." This was what the Chinese once called California.

"Now, if I blame you for my mistakes," Sam said, "and you blame someone else for yours, why that someone else has to blame somebody elser. Eventually, someone will be at the bottom of all that blame. I'm sorry to say that here and now, it's the Chinese. The Chinese are at the bottom of the blame, I believe, simply because those above them haven't taken the time to learn their language."

The questions stayed quiet inside Joan; the walking helped with that, the rolling hills, the clear sky. But Lee popped up with a good one.

"How did you know we're from San Francisco?" he asked.

"Ah, yes," Sam said. "Since you came through the lighthouse, I merely assumed."

"Go on," Joan called to Sam.

"To make sure those at the bottom of all this blame stay at the bottom, people give 'em a name or two. And you, Joan, are one of the 'Chinese Menace.' They are afraid of you, these fine upstanding citizens, and so will take any opportunity to harm you. Which is why most Chinese in San Francisco stay to their own world, Chinatown. Safer that way. Which is why you must keep your face hidden. If they find you and Lee together—a Chinese girl and a very white boy—I can only imagine how painful a discovery that might be."

"They wouldn't hurt me, would they?" Joan asked. She found her head sinking, her eyes glued to the rutted road.

"They would," Sam said, "and worse, I'm afraid. I'm telling no tall tale. Pinkie swear."

There was only the sound, for a while, of their feet on the dirt road.

Joan's parents often told her how difficult life in San Francisco had once been for the Chinese. They were discriminated against, forbidden citizenship, told they could not bring their families along. Sometimes they had been brutally attacked, even killed. "But we prevailed," her parents used to tell her. Joan had always believed these stories of Chinese struggle, but it was hard to *feel* that danger in her own San Francisco. Joan's San Francisco was more Chinese than not Chinese. They practically owned the joint.

But the tone in Sam's voice, the way he kept his head down, was enough to convince her, for now, that she should be wary. She set aside her questions; she wasn't sure she wanted any more answers.

"But why do they think the Chinese are such a menace?" Lee asked out of this silence. His voice was kind of shaky, a little thin.

"Because the Chinese are different than the people who hate them."

"That's stupid," Lee said. "Everybody's different."

Joan kept her eyes on her feet, on the road. She did not want to look up, did not want to see what she might find there.

"True enough, Lee," Sam said. "But that never stopped anyone from hatred. Why, I guarantee that in China, which is a land of many nations and peoples, there are Chinese who hate other Chinese, just for being different in some way. Even in these United States, some people so hate the *American* Negro for his differences that they keep him enslaved, refuse to see him as a human being. That's why we're fighting this war."

"Negro?" Lee said. "Do you mean African-American?"

From behind her, Joan could hear Sam pause.

"Why, yes," Sam said. "That would be a more civilized description."

The road had dipped down into a small valley but rose again, gently, and now the three of them stood atop another ridge, overlooking another, wider valley. Here the dairy farms and grass-covered hills gave way to grids of streets sparsely planted with one- and two-story houses and fenced-in yards. The houses were all brick or unpainted wood. Carriages, horses, people out and about—a quiet afternoon in this neighborhood.

On the far ridge, where they were headed, clusters of houses and more tightly packed streets spilled over from the other side, looking more like the San Francisco Joan knew. And from here, Joan could see the bay again. Three-masted sailing ships and squat smoke-belching steamships created a kind of watery traffic jam. There were even a few square-sailed Chinese junks.

Judging from the position of Alcatraz Island, a ways ahead of them, Joan figured they were pretty close to where Van Ness Avenue would one day be.

This was and was not San Francisco; it was beautiful if not a little confusing.

"Cooooool," Lee said, a long drawn out word.

"Cool?" Sam said. His version of the word was clipped, all wrong. "Why, son, it's baking today, hot as a dog's breath."

Sam was still behind them. His story of the Chinese Menace had kept them in their places.

Lee laughed. Joan wanted to.

"No, cooooool. Like awesome," Lee said.

"Ah. Indeed, it does fill one with a sense of awe. San Francisco, jewel of the Pacific."

"You could say that," Lee said.

"Cooooool," Sam said.

Joan could tell by the way Sam said this that he understood Lee's meaning of the word. Then she wondered when the word *cool* had become the word *cooooool*. It was nice to have something else to think about.

"Straight on," Sam said, and down the hill they went.

Now they were all quiet, even Sam. Joan thought this a very good idea. The streets were busier and busier with every block—men in dark suits, women in pouffy dresses. Strangers, fine upstanding citizens of San Francisco. Joan pulled her hat down as far as it would go.

"I hope you will have patience with my silence," Sam whispered into the hot day. "I shall, against my truest nature, endeavor to shut my yap."

Good, Joan thought, shut up shutting up already. Their shadows stretched long in front of them.

At the bottom of this valley was a broad intersection, near a stone steepled church, where they passed a pair of wooden street signs, crudely painted. Van Ness and Union, exactly where they should be. Joan looked up at Lee from under her hat's dark brim. WELL OKAY THEN.

When they began the steep climb to the next ridge, Joan couldn't have talked if she'd wanted to. They were all out of breath. Cars were so much a part of life in her San Francisco, she'd forgotten not only how many hills there were in the city but how steep.

By the time they reached the top of the ridge, the houses were more like the ones Joan was used to, all squeezed together, side by side, perched on slanting lots. There were wooden sidewalks now, steep but stepped. Lee was having a hard time keeping up; his Kixes kept poking out from under his dress.

At the top of Russian Hill, they could see over all of downtown San Francisco—North Beach and Chinatown and the Financial District. Or where they would be someday. But the tallest buildings here were three stories at the most, all brick and fresh looking. Along the waterfront, a forest of ships' masts and blocks of warehouses. Just like her San Francisco, this one was all hustle and bustle.

Across the bay, the hills were golden orange in the lowering sun. Joan saw where Berkeley ought to be, Oakland, too, though they seemed like villages more than cities. Mount Diablo's crooked profile hung purple farther east.

Sam gave Joan a little shove in the shoulder, and they started downhill again—San Francisco was all up and down—until Sam whispered, "Right. Here," and they traveled along Jones Street for a while, up and down, still high above North Beach and Chinatown. Oddly enough, the more people and carriages and horses that crowded the streets, the safer Joan felt. Lost in the crowd.

"Right again," Sam whispered again, and they zipped into a shadow-soaked alley. "Here," Sam said, more loudly now. They were hidden from the street by a stack of wooden crates.

"You live *here?*" Joan asked.

"Not here, no," Sam said, "but I would like, with your consent, to make another suggestion."

Joan and Lee nodded.

"My abode is far across town, near the waterfront, still a ways on. Our costumes have helped us avoid the soldiers, but with so many fine upstanding citizens be-tween us and our refuge, why, the danger is increased, especially should I be found imitating a Chinese servant. We'll be safer in the crowd if we look like the crowd. None of us should appear Chinese this close up, and besides, Master Lee here may be growing tired of his girlish appearance. Fine as it is."

Sam told them that around the corner was William Thompson, General Mercantile. Sam knew the owner a little, a very nosey man. They must stay together, he said, but Lee should conduct all their business. Joan and Sam would hang back for now, close but in the shadows. Safety was at issue. When he said the word "safety," Sam patted his ribs mysteriously.

They would need, they agreed, boy's shoes for Lee and for Joan, shoes and shirts, too, real shirts, not under-things, as Sam called their T-shirts. Hats, jack-ets. Sam reached under his Chinese shirt and handed Lee a hundred-dollar gold coin, a coin, he told them with a wicked smile, worth much more than its face value.

"We need a good story," Sam said. "In case Mr. Thompson finds himself too interested in our little party. I was thinking that—"

"Sam," Lee said, "I can handle it. I've got the story. Don't sweat it."

"Sweat it?" Sam said.

"Trust me," Lee said. "I'm thirteen—I know how to tell a story. It's part of my job."

"It's true," Joan said. "He's really good at lying." Joan, she wasn't so good, but Lee could stare down any adult and just start talking. Oh, he got caught now and then but rarely right away.

"I have made up my mind," Lee said, "that I shall never forget I am a girl." He batted his eyelashes and fanned himself with a pretend fan. He did make a fine young lady. "My name is Becky Thatcher, and my brother Tom is my dearest companion. Ain't that right, Tom honey?"

Lee's accent was a perfect model of Sam's.

William Thompson, General Mercantile, was standard Frontierland stuff. There was even a hitching post outside. Wooden shelves ran along the walls on which were displayed an odd assortment of goods—clothing and bolts of cloth, enameled kitchenware, odd iron tools. Five opened barrels took up most of the store—cheese, crackers, pickles, smelly dried fish, and what looked like meat packed in salt.

Joan stood with Sam just inside the front door. He kept his head bowed, invisible again. Joan figured, to be safe and because she was playing a boy, she'd hide in the shadows, too. Boys could do that, fold in on themselves. But Lee, as a girl, practically skipped to the front counter, where Mr. Thompson himself was waiting on two older women in bright pink dresses.

Mr. Thompson wore gartered sleeves, a clean white apron, and a handlebar mustache. He tore himself away from his customers.

"Good afternoon, miss," Mr. Thompson called in a falsely cheery voice. "What needs of yours might I meet this lovely day?"

Lee actually curtsied.

"Kind sir," Lee said, trilling, "I've come all the way from Monterey for your excellent goods. Which there are spoken of with the highest praise. My brother Tom and . . ."

Lee kept on talking, but Joan had to turn around and look out the high front windows of the store. She was trying to seem as disinterested as a teenage boy could but really just turning away from Lee before she exploded with laughter. Lee was really pouring it on and, frankly, just too good at being a girl.

Outside the window, a cowboy on a horse clopped by, holstered revolver and all. But so much more, too. A long, elegant carriage, purple with gold trim, clattered past, pink and white faces peering from its windows. Joan was surprised to find how much she could see from under her hat's brim and yet remain hidden. The people on the bus looked right at her, but she knew they didn't see her. She was invisible.

"Young man," the shopkeeper said, suddenly kneeling before Joan. "Your right foot, please."

The shopkeeper measured Joan's bare foot with a wooden contraption exactly like the metal contraptions used in the future. He looked up at Joan's face. Joan looked away, out the window.

"How's that for size?" the shopkeeper asked. Joan only mumbled—perfect boy talk.

"And another pair, please, but two sizes larger." Lee tittered girlishly. "My brother Tom, why, he grows like a weed."

Very clever of Lee, Joan realized. The larger size would fit him.

The shopkeeper disappeared into a backroom, returned to the counter where he wrapped their goods with brown paper, then tied the packages with white string.

"That'll be ten dollars and ninety-seven cents," the shopkeeper said.

Lee pushed the hundred dollar coin across the counter.

"Ah, very good," the shopkeeper said. "Alas, I do not have that much cash on hand, change-wise. But anyone in the possession of such wealth is surely worthy of this merchant's trust. It's clear yours is a family of means. To whom shall I charge this?"

Lee didn't skip a beat.

"To my father, of course," Lee said.

The women in pink, who had been carefully studying swatches of red-flocked wallpaper, suddenly looked up, interested.

"And your father is?" the shopkeeper asked.

"Why, Judge Thatcher. Of Monterey." Lee was doing the pretend fan bit again. Joan thought it a little much.

The women in pink, hearing this, looked at each other, nodding, then showered simpering smiles of approval on Lee.

"Ah, the judge, of course," the shopkeeper said.

"Thank you, kind sir." Lee reached, quite unladylike, for the bundles.

"Oh, no!" the shopkeeper protested. "Allow me."

Then he turned to Joan and Sam, who stood in the corner.

"You, boy!" the shopkeeper shouted, his voice thick with threat.

Joan froze. She'd been caught out.

"I said you!" the shopkeeper shouted, clearly speaking to Sam now. "China Man!"

The words "China" and "Man" had never sounded so sickening.

Sam moved forward, head bowed. The shopkeeper threw the bundles at him, as if trying to knock him over.

"Next time," he growled at Sam, "you be quicker when a white man speaks to you."

And again, the women in pink, those fine upstanding citizens, nodded their approval with well-rehearsed smirks.

Then the shopkeeper spit on Sam, the gob landing silver on his arm. "Good day, young Thatchers," he sang. "Please offer my respects to your father."

In the alley, Sam changed out of his Chinese shirt and hat. Lee slipped out of his dress and into his new shirt and shoes and jacket and hat. Sam stuffed the unwanted clothes into an empty barrel.

Though Joan only needed to put her new shoes over her old socks and her new shirt over her old one, she hid behind the stack of crates to get dressed. She had never felt so naked in her life.

SEVEN

The Street of Ships – The Funny Things Time Does – A Tale of the Great Unstuck – Smiggy McGlural

Life on a boat was good.

Lee kicked back from his empty plate and gazed out over the wooden railing at the placid bay waters. Above him, a thick throw of stars competed with the rising full moon to see which could offer the most light. The night was warm and still, everyone safely on board. Ah, this was living.

Granted, this boat—Sam insisted on calling it a ship—wasn't going anywhere, nor was it going anytime soon. The *Paul Jones* was parked back end first in the mud on the edge of Mission Bay. They were, Lee knew, close to where the Giants' baseball stadium would sit one day.

The *Paul Jones* was an old wooden steamship, one of a hundred other stranded ships lined up, hull by hull, along this stretch of the bay. The Street of Ships, Sam had explained, came into being because of the California Gold Rush. Fortune hunters from all over the world began arriving in San Francisco in 1849. When they arrived, these fortune hunters, along with the captains and crews they'd hired, abandoned their ships here, before heading up to goldfields, on foot and horseback, in search of untold riches.

The Street of Ships had became an unofficial neighborhood. Over time, these fortune hunters, returning to San Francisco empty-handed, occupied the deserted ships, owning them by possession. Squatters' rights. Sam had won the *Paul Jones* from its original squatter in a poker game back in May, the week he'd moved to San Francisco from Nevada. Sam's employer, the *San Francisco Morning Call*, provided a lovely suite for him at the Golden West Hotel, but finding the accommodations too fussy and crowded, Sam spent most of his nights on the *Paul Jones*. He'd practically grown up on riverboats, up and down the Mississippi, and felt more at home on water than land, he told Lee and Joan. Besides, Sam liked being "unfindable," as he put it, and liked the company down here. His fellow residents on the Street of Ships were the kind of folk who preferred life on the edge of society. Sam felt right at home.

And so did Lee. Sam's next-door neighbors, the Misses Greta and Penelope, had sent over a much needed dinner of cold cornpone, cold corned beef, and cold buttermilk. No meal had ever tasted better to Lee. The soldiers from Fort Point seemed only a bad memory now, Lee's feet were free of his stiff new shoes. Best of all, no one, for the moment, had to worry about Joan's safety or the menace presented by the fine upstanding citizens of San Francisco. They were all safe now. Yes, life on a boat was sweet.

Lee looked past the lighted oil lamp at Joan. She was sitting up, but her eyes were closed—safe enough to sleep? A trace of a smile hung about her mouth. Maybe she was just full—the girl could eat, no doubt about that. She'd set on their dinner with great ferocity.

Sam was at the bow of the *Paul Jones*, where it nosed into the bay. He was sitting on the boat's railing and patting his pockets casually, as if he'd lost something but couldn't quite remember what.

It had been such a hectic day, but now here on deck it was as if time had split open and there was a huge moment in which they could all breathe. Had time stopped or slowed or ceased to be at all?

Time had done a lot of funny things in the last twenty-four hours, and in this suspended moment, Lee let his mind wander about that notion.

First, there was that thing in his kitchen last night—did it count as last night if this was 1864?—where he'd stayed still and everyone else zoomed ahead into the future after his parents announced their divorce. Oh, yeah, that divorce thing. Then, of course, there was the Fort Point lighthouse and flying backwards 148 years. And after that, since Sam had shown up, everything went all rush-rush.

Even in this stillness, time continued to do funny things. Because even though so much had happened today, and they'd really only been aboard the *Paul Jones* for a relatively short time, Lee felt as though he'd been sitting here at this table forever.

When they were in the lighthouse, it felt to Lee as if they'd been there forever, too, and always would be. Same was true of the cliff, the creek, the farmhouse, the city's steep streets—Lee had thought they'd never get to the top of Union—and the general store, where that man had spit on Sam because he thought Sam was Chinese. Each of these moments felt like the only moment that would ever exist.

It was weird. Lee had always assumed time was pretty

regular, consistent, moving forward like the hands of a clock. But from here, the day seemed all chopped up, more like a bunch of photographs than a movie. Lee knew that the journey across San Francisco was one long take—the sun setting lower and lower and finally disappearing proved that—but all he could recall now was a series of images, each one of which had felt eternal at the time.

Walking away from the general store, Joan and Lee in their new clothes, Sam flipping his one-hundred-dollar gold coin, telling Joan and Lee that this trick worked every time. The struck look on Joan's face, how she seemed to be standing a million miles away from everyone. Lee saying, "Sam, uh, Joan," Lee frightened out of his wits for her, Sam picking up the cue, moving them on.

At one street corner, two men had drawn pistols on each other, and Sam scurried Lee and Joan away. Lee realized in that moment how many other fine upstanding citizens wore guns, almost all the men. Those two drawn guns had allowed him to see all the other guns.

Lee could not be sure of the order of these images, but at some point, Joan had suddenly ducked into a bookstore. A. Roman, Books, Inc., since 1853—Lee could still see the painted window. Sam and Lee had followed Joan in, and there she was, holding up a newspaper, pointing to the date, September 6, 1864.

Then, maybe somewhere near Geary Street, a broken down, deserted shack right next to a brand-new opera house, the Argonaut, all fancy pink marble and gold angels hanging above.

Four men, obviously drunk, sleeping together in front of a white church.

Joan, her head bowed, her face hidden. But she was talking, talking, though Lee now had a hard time remembering anything anyone said during that part of their journey.

The traffic on Market Street, just like in 2012, except it was all horses and carriages. And the billowing black plume of a steam train down the center of Market. The crowds. One big picture of all that, which might have been a million little pictures smooshed together. A kind of living painting.

The Street of Ships, blue in the evening, the yellow oil lamps from the portholes of the other ships—this part of the day was cool but scary, and it, too, seemed to last forever.

The weirdest thing of all—where was this? Lee couldn't remember. Turning to look behind him, at some silent signal, Lee spotted a stranger, all dressed in black.

He was waving at Lee and had just opened his mouth to speak when suddenly, he evaporated. Not there anymore. The image stayed with Lee, that stranger, half there and half not there. It freaked Lee out, and he was going to say something to Joan about the stranger, but she had plenty to be freaked out about already.

And then they were at the stern of the *Paul Jones*, and Sam was welcoming them to his "humblest of abodes." They climbed a rickety ladder and were on board, and everyone sighed. Safe at last.

Sitting there on deck, time did yet one more funny thing. Lee realized that the time it had taken him to recall all these images, to string them together and question them, had been less than an instant.

Then time started up again and moved forward. Sam found what he was looking for in his pocket. He pulled out a corncob pipe and struck a match on his boot heel. He puffed on the pipe.

"Sam," Joan hissed at him. "Are you kidding me?"

Sam startled, then bowed deeply to Joan.

"I am desolated, as the French say." He was patting his pockets again. "I don't know where my hospitality has fled. May I offer you a pipe?" He pulled a second corncob from his jacket.

"What?" Joan practically screeched. "Are you crazy? We're just kids."

Sam was shocked.

"No intent to offend," he said.

"Don't you know," Joan said, "that smoking is bad for you? No one should smoke. Ever."

Lee was glad to see Joan riled up; it meant she was herself again. But he did hope she wouldn't go all "matter of principle" on Sam. She had a thing about principles that could be pretty annoying.

"Oh, my," Sam said. "I've always held out great hope for the future, but this is disappointing news. Smoking is bad for you? How am I to tell a story without my pipe?"

Joan sat back down.

"If you must," she said. "But breathe that way."

The pipe had gone out. Sam struck another match on his boot heel and puffed the pipe to life.

"Very well," Sam said. "I shall regale you with my Tale of the Great Unstuck." He turned to Lee. "Now that I know the stories of how you came unstuck— about the awful fractures in your families' lives and the desert of a future awaiting you both—you ought to know mine. Perhaps by comparing them, we might find the path to get you two home."

It was obvious Lee had missed a big old something along the way, had missed out on a lot of talking. When had Joan told Sam their stories? Wow, he'd really zoned out. He kind of wished he'd been able to tell his own story.

Rather than ask for a do-over, though, he figured he'd concentrate on listening. He was used to catching up like this at school.

Lee took a big chug of buttermilk. Whoever would have thought buttermilk would be good? But it was thick and tangy, such a surprise to his tongue. If anyone had told him yesterday that . . . oops. He'd better start listening.

"Like you both," Sam was saying, "I didn't care one whit for the future I saw for myself. I, Sam Clemens, had come to San Francisco—via the Nevada Territory, via Hannibal, Missouri, which is on the great Mississippi—to make a new future. I was only twenty-eight years old and wasn't quite sure what that future would be, but like a million others, I reckoned San Francisco, having very little past to it, was a good place to start over."

Lee stared out at the black waters of the bay. The moon laid a silver path across its surface. It helped him to focus on Sam's story by looking, not at Sam, but at the bigger world.

"Arriving here, with only my hundred-dollar gold coin, I applied for a position with that most disreputable institution, the newspaper. I had done some scribbling for a Nevada paper, and Mr. George Barnes of the *San Francisco Morning Call*, rather than interpret my journalism experience as grounds for insanity, hired me on, instead, as a writer of what we hacks call lokulitems."

Sam said this last word as one, but Lee teased out both words—*local items*.

"I took on this most onerous of tasks. I wrote what our readers most wanted to read. Reviews of plays readers did not care about and the scandalous lives of their actors, about which they seemed to care a great deal. I penned reviews of restaurants where the food served was bland though the fashions were rather spicy. I reported on heinous crimes, crimes committed by outlaws and elected officials both, stories whose only moral seemed to be that crime might actually pay and pay well."

"Sam!" Joan said through her teeth. "The Great Unstuck?"

CHILLAX was the LOOK Lee aimed at Joan.

"I shall proceed," Sam said, and he lit his pipe again. His words and his smoke rose up into the night sky. "Silly as those lokulitems were, the writing bug had caught me, bit me hard on the ankle and wouldn't let go. Therefore, I made the error of imagining I could write something important, something with meaning.

Something I might dare to call literature. I wrote story after story about matters I perceived as urgent and time- less. Corruption in our city hall. The malfeasance of bankers. Poverty and despair among our downtrod- den masses. Relations between the races. I wrote— wishfully—stories about injustice and the need for justice and our seeming incapacity to find justice."

Lee was listening with both ears now.

"And every one of those stories was put to rest on the standing galley, rejected by my editor. Now, it must be said that Mr. George Barnes is, despite being a news- paper editor, a man of fine intelligence and philosophy. Still, as an editor, it is his job to, shall we say, shape the truth. He rejected my more ambitious writing on the principle that it did not pay. Our readers part with twelve and one half cents a week for their subscrip- tions, and they want, Barnes informed me, nothing of my grand ambition. They want no more truth than they pay for."

Sam emptied his pipe on his boot heel, put it back in his pocket.

"I wanted to write, but the newspaper business stood between me and what I wanted to say. I turned my back on the future; I could not imagine what mine would be like. For two months, I walked this city as a ghost of sorts. I was in limbo. Until one day."

Sam allowed a small tide of silence to sweep over the *Paul Jones*.

"Then what?" Joan whispered. She was no longer impatient with Sam, Lee heard in her voice. She simply wanted the story to continue.

"I found myself in that lighthouse. Like yourselves. The keeper of that lighthouse, old Wickie, was a frequent poker companion of mine, and he and the other soldiers would look the other way and allow me to use it as a ponderin' place. And so, there I was, yesterday, September fifth, 1864, ponderin' how dismal my future was, when I fell asleep like you and, like you, I woke up in a time other than my own."

Joan leaped in. "Where were you? I mean, when?"

Sam patted his pocket for his pipe, but refrained. "Like you, I wound up here in San Francisco. But it's harder to say when. It was in the past, I know that, long before the lighthouse. I awoke on the bay's shore, where Fort Point stands today. Above me stood the original Spanish outpost. My Spanish is not quite that good, so I fled, tried to gather my wits.

"No sooner had I found a cozy bluff to hide behind, I was rousted by a Spanish soldier, who gave chase. A musket ball blew so close past my ear, I doubt a page of the family Bible would fit between the two. In true heroic manner, I continued to run, only to stumble on a large but rather well camouflaged stone. When I stood up, the world had changed again. Oh, still our fair city, but much changed. The year was 1910, I would discover. It was a world more hospitable to myself but filled with such righteous wonders—horseless carriages, a flying machine, what I learned to call the telephone."

Sam's story had drawn them in. Neither Joan nor Lee interrupted.

"I stayed in 1910 for some weeks, learning more about the advance of time than I cared to. Then I came unstuck again. And yet again, and yet again. At least half a dozen occasions, I believe, moving up and down the river of time but always moored in San Francisco. Until yesterday, when I came back to my own time, September the fifth, 1864."

"How long were you gone?" Lee asked.

"How did you get back?" Joan asked.

They spouted these questions simultaneously.

"More than a month," Sam said, "if I calculated correctly. As for getting back, I'm not quite sure. I was walking down Montgomery Street in 1892 when I simply came unstuck again, or in this case, restuck, in my own time. These unstickings are unnerving at first, but one gets used to them."

"Used to them?" Lee asked.

"You really don't have a clue, do you?" Joan asked. "You have no idea how we get back."

Both questions arrived simultaneously again, though in quieter tones.

"Not yet I don't, no," Sam said. He seemed very sorry to say this. "I was headed to Fort Point today to see if I might learn more. That's when I found you."

A new silence enclosed the deck of the *Paul Jones*. A tired silence, Lee felt, an end-of-day silence, enormous.

Sam puffed on his pipe. Joan stared into the oil lamp's yellow flame. Lee struggled to keep his eyes open.

"So, what do we do now?" Joan asked quietly.

"I reckon what's best," Sam said, "is sleep. There's secure quarters for you both belowdecks."

Sleep. What a wonderful word. Lee realized there was only so much freaking out a person could do in one day. If green-and-red polka-dotted wombats suddenly started dancing across the deck of the *Paul Jones*, Lee was certain he'd only yawn.

Time had fallen back into place. Lee felt the shape of the day return.

"Sleep, yes," Joan said. "We can start again in the morning. Figure this out." Joan's words slurred.

Whatever sound first spooked Sam, Lee didn't hear

it until after Sam had leaped across the deck, blown out the oil lamp, and frozen them all in place.

Then Lee heard it, the creaking of the ladder at the stern of the *Paul Jones*. Someone was boarding the ship.

Sam kept them silent and in place with his hands and his eyes, got them to hide below the deck's dining table. He rose and plastered himself against the wall of the pilot house. From his vest pocket, he pulled a tiny silver pistol. A derringer, Lee knew. It gleamed in the moonlight. Sam cocked the derringer.

Whoever had boarded the *Paul Jones* was creaking towards the bow.

The instant the figure stepped out of the shadows, Sam thrust the gun into the stranger's belly and shouted, "Varmint!"

The stranger froze, visible now, but he smiled at Sam. Then Sam did a crazy little dance; he tore the hat off the stranger's head and stomped on it repeatedly, shouting "Smiggy, Smiggy, Smiggy!"

"Evenin', Mr. Twain, sir," the stranger said.

Sam stomped on the stranger's hat again. Vehemently.

"Smiggy!" Sam yelled. "Are you trying to get yourself killed, you mud-sucking catfish?"

Sam uncocked the pistol and pocketed it, then shook his head.

"Everyone," Sam said with a sigh, "may I present Mr. Smiggy McGlural, one of the *Call's*, how shall I say it, more recent employees."

Joan and Lee rose up from the table.

Smiggy seemed delighted rather than frightened. As if he'd just been caught in a game of hide-and-seek. Even in the dark, Lee saw that Smiggy had bright red hair and really big ears.

"Mr. Twain, sir," Smiggy said, unable to hide his raucous smile. "I've been looking all over for you. Mr. Barnes sent me. He told me to tell you, you were being followed."

Twain?

"I know that, Smiggy," Sam said. "I'm being followed by *you*."

"Oh, no, sir," Smiggy said. "It's those Irish butchers, Mr. Twain. They found out about your story, the China Man one. Mr. Barnes says they want to shut you up. Came to the *Call* looking for you. Messed it up a bit, too."

Lee did not at all like that the word "butchers" was so close to those ugly words "China Man."

"But Barnes didn't print the story," Sam said.

"They heard about it still," Smiggy said, "and don't want their reputations harmed. Anyway, I looked all over for you. You are a slippery one. I guess a reporter's got to be slippery, huh, Mr. Twain?"

Twain. That name again. Joan and Lee looked at each other. VE-RY INTERESTING.

Sam shook his head.

"Tell Barnes thanks for me. Now go home, Smiggy. Pretend you did not find me."

"Yes, sir, but beggin' pardon, sir, I did find you, sir. You're right here in front of me."

"No, Smiggy," Sam said, leaning into him. "You never did find me, see? And you never heard of the *Paul Jones*, neither. But you did hear that I had run myself out of town on a Chilean timber freighter, yes? And you've never ever seen my companions."

"But, Mr. Twain, sir . . ."

Sam put his finger to his nose, tapped it twice.

"Oh," Smiggy said, "I got you now. A reporter's ruse, eh? Shall I keep writing your lokulitems for you then?"

"Please, Smiggy, do," Sam said, smiling. "We'll confuse 'em all that way."

Lee thought Smiggy might faint.

"Honestly, truly, Mr. Twain, sir?"

Smiggy nodded. Well, he hadn't stopped nodding.

"Good. Now, vamoose," Sam said. "And remember, you've seen nothing."

Smiggy turned and scooted to the rear of the *Paul Jones*, disappearing down the ladder.

"That boy is about perfect for a reporter," Sam said to Lee and Joan. "Has the right amount of brains for it."

INFORMATION OVERLOAD seemed the only appropriate LOOK for Lee and Joan to share at that moment, a sort of we-drank-too-much-caffeine kind of stare.

And then time did one more funny thing that night. Lee had thought the day was coming to a close finally, had felt it in his bones. But, no, all thoughts of sleep had gone. The moon rode full and high in the sky. It might be midnight; it might even be the next day. Lee couldn't figure out exactly when it was, but he knew for sure that this very long day was far from over.

EIGHT

Witches and Ha'ants –
Further Tales of the Great Unstuck –
A Very Long Distance Phone Call –
Tight Quarters and a Ticking Clock

Joan had been about to roll off the top of awake and into a big box of sleep and, man, did she need it. How long was this day anyway? One hundred and forty-eight years? Negative 148 years? How did you count backwards time? She'd definitely need her graphing calculator for this one.

Sleep would have been great, but, no, there was that Smiggy guy, and then Sam's gun and those words— *butchers? China Man? Twain?* I mean, seriously. So much for sleep. Joan was wide awake again. Tired but awake. Her eyeballs felt funny.

Lee looked like his eyeballs felt funny, too.

Sam was busy doing that string thing he'd done back at the lighthouse. He wrapped that ratty old piece of string around a lock of his hair, then spun in a circle three times, muttering under his breath.

"Superstitious much?" Joan said. Not only did her eyeballs feel funny, her voice sounded funny. And not ha-ha funny, either.

"Ain't no superstition about it," Sam said. "Proven protection against witches and ha'ants. This is no night for taking chances." Sam looked up at the blazing full moon. He rapped the table three times with his knuckles.

"Ha'ants?" Joan said.

"Spirits. Ghosts. Anything that'll ha'ant you."

Sam was being *very* serious.

"So, this ship is 'ha'anted'?" Joan asked. A little laugh ran through her words.

"Not anymore," Sam said.

He pulled the string from his hair, folded it into his fist, blew on it, then put it back in his pocket. Sam was *super-serious* now.

"You know that's crazy. Right?" Joan said.

"Perhaps," Sam said. "But it might also be crazy to *not* believe in what you can't see or explain simply because you can't see or explain it. I find it reassuring to protect myself against what I can't see. I belong to the

Church of Knockwood." Sam rapped the table three times again.

"Fine, whatever," Joan said, "but seriously, what—"

Lee's voice leaped out of nowhere.

"Sam," Lee was suddenly saying, "just shut up, okay. I mean, what was that guy talking about, Smurfy or whatever his name was? What butchers? What China Man? And how come he kept calling you Mr. Twain? You said your name was Clemens."

Something in Lee's voice got to her, and Joan exploded, too. "Yeah, Sam, or whoever you are. Tell us everything right now. All of it. I'm kind of freaking out here."

"Freaking out?" Sam asked.

"Yeah," she said, "you know, like, totally freaked out. Like, I'm gonna lose it and start hurting people."

Sam himself looked freaked out. "Do not be freaking out," he said. "I'll tell you everything. I'd planned to but was waiting for the right time. Sometimes—"

"Every. Thing. Right. Now." Joan's voice was dangerous, even she heard that.

"I will, I swear, but it takes time. That's one of the reasons we have time. It keeps everything from happening at once. The big picture, that takes time. Stories take time. Please, have a seat. Let me try again."

Lee and Joan traded THIS BETTER BE GOOD. They sat at the table, while Sam went to the bow, and puffed up another dream of pipe smoke. The oil lamp stayed dark; moonlight would do.

"The butchers, a Chinese man out shopping for his family's dinner, and Mr. Mark Twain, the celebrated author, these are all bound to the same story, the story I began to tell you earlier. But allow me to revise."

Mr. Mark Twain? *The* Mark Twain? This would take every ounce of Joan's patience. But where else was she going to go? She leaned back in her chair, breathed deeply.

Sam puffed up his words and his smoke.

"I arrived in San Francisco in May, 1864. After a youth of dreaming on the banks of the mighty Mississippi, I had gone off to the Nevada Territory to seek my fortune in silver. While I lost several fortunes there, I never gained a single one, and so—"

No, this would not do.

"Sam!" Joan squeaked. "Get to it. The truth."

"Ah, yes. The tale our friend Smiggy referred to, the butchers and the Chinese gentleman. This took place only last Saturday, September the third. As I told you, I had already become disenchanted with my journalistic duties, and on that day, as I had done so many days, I simply wandered, Smiggy doing all my work instead.

"I found myself on Kearny Street, just after noon. I had paused, as is my wont, to lean against a lamppost to light my pipe, when a scuffle erupted a few shop fronts down the way. I squeezed to the front of the crowd—using a reporter's best weapon, my rather sharp elbows—only to find the most revolting sight I have come across in all my twenty-eight years."

Sam set his pipe down. His voice was different now. He seemed to be speaking more to himself than to an audience.

"The sight I saw was this: An Irish butcher, whom I knew a little by reputation, had taken offense at the manner in which a Chinese customer had ordered his half a pound of tripe. They deemed his manner, I heard them say, 'disrespectful.' Incensed by this disrespect, the Irish butcher and four of his good friends beat this Chinese man to within the last hair of his life. He was punched, kicked, and sliced with a meat cleaver. I cannot bear to detail more of his injuries. Gruesome."

Joan could see the street where this had happened, could see the man on the ground, surrounded by a cloud of hatred. The same hatred, only amplified, she'd seen in the general store, when the shopkeeper spit on Sam.

"But happily, or so I thought," Sam went on, "one of San Francisco's finest, a police officer, was standing a few yards hence. When I pointed out that a man was being brutally disinvited from the planet, the policeman's only response was that he didn't see nothin', now did he? The policeman twirled his nightstick and continued to watch the beating, as if it were a sporting match on which he'd placed a wager."

Lee and Joan looked at each other. SHUDDER.

"I appealed to the onlookers and moved to stop this horror, but the fine upstanding citizens held me back. Then it was over. The butcher in his bloody apron spit on the Chinese man as a last insult and, laughing with his companions, fairly waltzed away. The sole Samaritan, I moved to help the man, but a crowd of his own people appeared and carted him off to the safety of Chinatown."

Joan looked down at her hands, her Chinese hands.

"That man," Lee said, "did he, I mean . . ."

"He lives," Sam said, turning to them both. "To the best of my knowledge. I know I prayed for him, and I rarely pray." Sam fiddled with his pipe.

"But," Lee asked, "what does it have to do with Mark Twain?"

"Part two will now commence," Sam said. He stood in the bow, as if he were the lookout. "I thought I had given up on my future, but not fully, it turned out. This, I thought, this horrible story of the butchers and the man they nearly killed, this was a story that deserved—no, *needed*—to be told. I came straight back here and wrote that story for the *Morning Call*. I knew its truth could not be denied."

Far off, a steamship's whistle sounded low and plaintive, and after its bellow died, the silence on the deck of the *Paul Jones* was even thicker.

Joan whispered for Sam to continue.

"But that story, too, was rejected, with a simple editorial note: 'Nothing about the Chinese.' As if the horror of that night could simply be erased. When I saw those words, my despair increased. If the world would not heed this truth, why write at all? The next day is when I came unstuck in the lighthouse."

An OH flashed between Joan and Lee.

"And that is why I did not want to tell you this story, Joan. It's dangerous enough for you here. But now, Smiggy says, that butcher wants to *disrespect* me. And I fear I've placed you in great danger."

Sam's voice cracked.

Joan was divided. A part of her wished Sam had not told this story at all. But another part of her was glad he had. The truth was hard to look at, but it was better to know.

"Mark Twain?" Lee asked. "You said . . ."

"Ah, yes," Sam said, as if he were waking from a confusing dream. "Mr. Twain. As promised. When I came unstuck my second time, I found myself again in San Francisco. As I said, it was the year 1910.

"Now, 1910 marks the return of Halley's Comet, which comes around every seventy-five or so years and is considered a sign of . . . well, it's considered a sign of many things. I happened to be born in 1835, during the time of Halley's last visit. So, I take the comet to be a sign of good fortune.

"Having adjusted somewhat to coming unstuck, I set off into the city, not only to see the wonders of the future, but to see if the comet had returned as promised. And it had."

Sam's voice was quiet, intent.

"The day's papers were full of the comet, photos and such. The date was April 22, 1910. The height of the comet's glory had passed, but it seemed I might still see it that night, if somewhat faded. And I did see the comet that night and it was breathtaking.

"But there was another story that occupied the front pages of the newspapers that day. It seems the country, nay, the world, was mourning the loss of its most beloved writer—man by the name of Mark Twain, a figure of great fame, and, they said, great fortune."

The world grew still, absolutely still. Even the waves stopped their gentle lapping.

"You might have knocked me over with a goose feather. I knew the name Mark Twain. It's an old riverboat call, you see. 'Mark Twain' is what's hollered when a depth of two fathoms is reached. I also knew that one young man had chosen that call as his writerly pen name. And I knew it, because I was that young man. When Smiggy called me Twain, he did so because I write under that name for the *Morning Call*."

Joan looked at Lee. wow.

"One paper showed a photograph of me from San Francisco, in 1864, this very time and place. How do you not recognize yourself? And the last nail in that coffin—so to speak—was this tidbit: Twain was born during Halley's appearance, and so did he die then, too. I was Twain. Or am. Or will be. Or might.

"It was both a wonder and a dread to find myself reading my own obituary. Rumors of my death seemed exaggerated on that day."

"*You* wrote *Huckleberry Finn* and *Tom Sawyer?*" Lee asked, practically giggling.

"So they say."

Joan was watching Sam carefully. She expected his face to be all sparkly. After all, he was claiming that he would become Mark Twain, a great American writer, a famous person. Instead, every time he said the name Twain, his face scrunched into a dark knot.

"Duuuude!" Lee said. "You're Mark Twain?"

"Dude?" Sam said.

"Yeah," Lee said. "You know, *duuuude!*"

"Dude."

"No," Lee said, "it's more like *duuuude!*"

"What is a dude?"

"Well," Lee said. "I'm a dude. You're a dude. Joan, she's definitely a dude. It's all how you say it, when you say it. It's just dude. As in 'Yo, dude, what was that like, finding out you were Mark Twain?'"

"Dude, it was awesome," Sam said, "but I was also freaking the out."

"Just freaking out."

"And I was."

Joan was trying to put these things together in her brain, but it was hard. "Are you telling us the truth?" This was all Joan wanted to know.

"As I know it," Sam said. He reached into his vest pocket and pulled out something small and shiny. "You have been asked to believe a good deal today, a good deal for which there seems to be no explanation. Mayhap, this will help."

He dropped something into Joan's hand. It was a coin,

a dime, but one Joan had never seen. It bore on its face the profile of a woman wearing a crown; and around the edge, a circle of stars. At the bottom, fresh and clear, the date 1910.

Joan bit the dime. People always did that in movies. Ow. Certainly felt genuine. No, it was genuine.

NOW WHAT? was the LOOK she'd composed for Lee, but Lee was staring at Sam, the blush of his "dude" enthusiasm gone.

"Is Joan safe here?" Lee said. "Tonight? Should we leave?"

"Safe as houses," Sam said. "Smiggy won't give us up. Not yet at least."

Joan turned around and stared into the city's lights, the shadowy buildings.

"But," was all Lee seemed capable of saying.

"Tomorrow," Joan said. "Tomorrow we need to make some plan to get out of here. Get back to where we once belonged."

"Exactly," Sam said.

Sam gave them each an oil lamp—whale oil!—then led them down a narrow ladder into the ship's dark hold. Joan had expected the captain's quarters to be a bit more palatial—she'd watched too many pirate movies. The captain's "bedroom," as Sam called it, was nothing more than a high closet with a thin mattress on the bottom of it. The living quarters, where Lee would sleep, was simply a small table surrounded on three sides by upholstered benches, a room about the size of the entrance hall in her family's home.

The doors to both the living quarters and the bedroom were ironclad and impenetrable in the event of a mutiny.

Sam would sleep on the bench in the pilot house, and when he said this, he gave them a left-handed glance, patting the pocket of his vest where he kept his derringer.

"Time to hang fire," Sam said. "Lock the doors behind me."

Lee tossed his backpack into a corner, then plopped down on the padded bench, pulled a striped blanket over him. Joan snugged feetfirst into the bedroom, cramped but cozy.

This was the first time since the lighthouse they'd been alone together. So much to say. Joan's head hung out the narrow door, right above where Lee's head rested on a gold-tasseled pillow. This was like hanging out at Lee's house, Joan on the couch and Lee on the floor, and all their talk-talk.

They tried to reassure each other that what they

thought happened today had happened. Did you see this? What about that? Remember when? The whole day, from the lighthouse to the *Paul Jones*. The changed and unchanged city, the soldiers, the farmhouse, the Chinese Menace. The shocking news that their tour guide in the Great Unstuck was none other, he claimed, than the famous writer Mark Twain.

Joan and Lee had both read *Tom Sawyer* in seventh and *Huck Finn* this year. Back then—whenever that was—they had agreed these were their favorite school books of all time. *Tom* and *Huck* were funny books, and as part of an extra-credit project, Lee and Joan had spent a week or so concocting their own raft journey down the Mississippi, making plans to escape all the stupid stuff that "civilization" had to offer.

Lee suggested maybe this was why they'd come unstuck, their raft project, the Twain factor. Maybe they'd thought too hard about it. Joan was skeptical.

"Do you really think he's Mark Twain?" she asked.

Lee looked up at her, upside down.

"Well, Twain's real name *was* Sam Clemens," he said, "and he *was* a pilot on the Mississippi, and I remember he *was* in San Francisco for a while."

Apparently Lee did pay attention in school.

"Really?" she said. "You really think so?"

Lee pitched her a soft and assuring WHY NOT? And

in that WHY NOT? much was said. They were here, in 1864, on a ship. Why not Mark Twain, too?

They were quiet for what seemed a long time. Joan had one other thing she wanted to talk about, but she was afraid to bring it up. Still, she had to.

"I saw something else today," she said. "Something I didn't tell you about."

The timbers of the *Paul Jones* creaked loudly.

"I saw this man," she said. "When we were back at the fort. He was all dressed in black, and he was waving at us, I think. And then he disappeared. Pfft."

"No way!" Lee said. "I saw someone just like that, when we were coming across town, in an alley. And he just—pfft!"

"Who do you think it was?" Joan asked.

"Someone else who's come unstuck. There could be more of us."

"Maybe."

"Did he scare you?" Lee asked.

"A little, but not really. He was waving."

"We should ask Sam," Lee said.

Joan was suddenly thinking about her family, about how impossibly far away her world seemed.

"We *will* get back," Lee said. "I know it."

Joan loved him for saying this. She knew Lee had no idea really *if* they'd get back, much less *how*, but he said it anyway, and it helped. He seemed to believe what he was saying.

"It's too bad we can't call," he said then, "and let the 'rents know we'll be late for dinner. Like a hundred and forty-eight years late."

Joan's hand reached automatically for her backpack. She felt like a well-trained dog; she had heard the word phone and reached for it.

"E.T. phone home," Lee said in his funny E.T. voice. Joan had to laugh. This was what they always said at "phone checks," those times when their parents demanded they call "just to check in."

Joan rummaged through her backpack and pulled out her candy-apple-red Kookie phone. Joan saw this phone a million times a day, but right now it looked significantly strange.

When the phone flipped open, the touch screen glowed to life, a bright and sharp blue light that filled the captain's quarters. The oil lamps were no match for this machine.

Joan punched in her home number. What if her mom did pick up? That would mean things were even weirder than they already were. Joan kind of hoped that the phone lady voice would come on: "We're sorry, the space-time continuum you're attempting to reach is out of network."

She pressed CALL. The display read "Calling Mom" for a few seconds, then "Dropped Call." She hit REDIAL; "Dropped Call" again. The time and date stamp on the screen showed blinking 8's. Lee was sitting up now, both of them hunched over the Kookie phone.

With a swipe of her finger, the Web browser came up. They were not connected to the Internet.

Joan put her finger over the PHOTOBOOK icon, paused before touching it. When she touched it, her album sprang to life. Lee leaned over and touched the first picture. Joan had taken this picture of the two of them, her arm extended. They had just finished a chocolate binge, both of them delirious and messy in Joan's kitchen.

They zoomed through the pictures—swipe, swipe, swipe. The City School's deserted playground on a rainy day. Lee waiting in line for fresh Eggette waffles in Glen Park. Joan's brothers and sisters fighting about something at the dinner table, everyone's mouth open, except for Joan's mom's—she was smiling off to one side. Joan at Lee's house, jumping high off of his couch. Last year's Halloween on Belvedere Street, when Joan had gone as a purple crayon and Lee a tree made of old stuffed animals. Picture after picture showed their lives. Joan kept expecting to break down and sob—summer camp homesick—but no, no tears.

The battery was fading. It beeped its little alarm. And then the screen went black. The phone was dead. There would be no getting back any of that past.

"So—" Joan said, but Lee was asleep. She pulled his blanket over him, blew out the lamp, and scrunched down into her captain's bed, closing the door only partway.

In the dim light of her own lamp, she examined a low shelf at her side. There was a short stack of Sam's books— *The Adventures of King Arthur, Robinson Crusoe, One Thousand and One Nights, The Canterbury Tales, Shakespeare's Comedies*. On another shelf was a black leather-bound notebook and a cache of rough-looking pencils. If Sam was Mark Twain, then . . . No, she would not open it. Her brother Newton had once read her diary— "Jo-an's got a boyfriend"—and that was something no one should ever do, snoop in someone else's writing.

There was also a square clock in a brass case, a little key sticking out of it. Joan wound it up, and it commenced to ticking. Each tick of the second hand was exactly like all the others. Time was moving forward, unstoppable. How did you unwind a clock? You didn't. Time went forward. Even 148 years in the past, time moved forward.

She stared at the clock's face, watching the seconds proceed and pulling the minute hand along behind.

She blew out the lamp and lay back in the dark. But the second hand continued to tick.

Her last thought before drifting off was, Hold it, if Sam can go into *his* future, see who he will be, then it only makes sense . . .

NINE

The Good Old Days –
A Flock of Angry Birds –
The Misses Greta
and Penelope – Back to the Future?

You know what? Lee liked it here in the past.

Sometimes in books and movies, when characters woke up in strange beds, they went through this whole "Gee, where am I?" routine. But when Lee opened his eyes this morning, he saw the varnished wooden ceiling of the captain's quarters, felt the warm sun that baked the room, heard Joan's soft snoring above him, and knew exactly where he was, and when. And loved it.

This was still 1864, this was Sam's ship, the *Paul Jones*, and everything was still old-timey San Francisco. Over a century before his parents' divorce and a high school life without Joan. Lee liked this past so much he figured maybe he would just stay here.

"You up?" Lee whispered into the quiet cabin, but Joan didn't rouse. Joan could be kind of a boy sometimes— one of the reasons Lee liked her so much. She could eat like a horse, way beyond what Lee could stuff down. And she often slept on weekends until way past noon. Lee had spent long Saturday hours in Joan's living room, waiting for her to wake up so they could go do whatever they had planned for that day. One thing you never wanted to do was wake her up before she was ready. That could get ugly.

Up on deck, Sam was sitting near the bow, a fishing pole wedged into his chair's rungs. Lee was surprised to discover it was later than he'd imagined. The sun was directly overhead.

"Mornin', Master Lee," Sam called through teeth clenched around his pipe's stem. "Drag up a sittin' chair and let's get you a line in the water. Fishing is best with two. You don't catch any more fish, but then that's never been the point of fishing."

The pole Sam gave Lee was nothing more than a straight piece of bamboo. There was no reel, just a long piece of string with a bent nail for a hook. The bait of the day: chunks of dry salami.

"What are we fishing for?" Lee asked.

"Pleasure," Sam said, and he tossed Lee's makeshift hook overboard. "A sure catch."

They sat in the warm sunshine and "fished," and the sun felt great on Lee's bare feet. Lee remembered that the summer he was eight, he and his dad "took up" fishing. Several times they'd gone out to Lake Merced with their brand-new poles and spent the day there. They caught a fish or two along the way, but what Lee remembered most were the bags of sandwiches they'd devoured for lunch, the two of them together on the lake's shore.

Sam pointed out the various watercraft that crowded the bay—water taxis, schooners, freighters, ferries. He showed Lee his own small sailboat, which was wedged into the mud below the bow of the *Paul Jones*. Sam used this boat when life on shore got too "complexifyin'."

Every once in a while, a steamship would hoot, and from the city, a steam train would answer that call.

Sam wanted to know *everything* about the future, so Lee described his day-to-day life in 2012. Go to school all day, do homework all evening, go to sleep: repeat. Sam was fascinated by the machines that governed Lee's life—cars, televisions, computers, cell phones. But he was also appalled by the shape of Lee's existence. Was school so important? Did Lee never hook out of school, spend the day in butterfly idleness, barefoot and free?

"Never," Lee said. "I'd get in major trouble."

"By hokey," Sam said. "Again, the future disappoints."

Sam had a point. From where Lee sat, his feet propped on the ship's railing, a baited hook in the water, the afternoon stretching ahead, the past seemed a perfect place.

Every once in a while, Lee or Sam would pull their hooks out of the water, only to find the bait firmly attached. Fishing at its finest.

About an hour later, Joan emerged from belowdecks. She was wide awake and rarin' to go.

"Okay, you two," she barked. "Let's get going. We've got to get back to the future."

So forceful was Joan's approach that Lee tipped backwards in his chair, splat on the deck. Sam's pipe went flying overboard.

"Whoa!" Sam called.

"Jeez," Lee said. "Give a guy a chance."

"No," she said, her hands on her hips. "No time, no time for any of that. We've got to have a plan. You promised, Sam."

"I don't know," Lee said, "I kind of like it here."

"You want to stay here?" Joan said. "That is plain crazy. You can't possibly mean it."

It happened in an instant. Joan was suddenly up in Lee's face, inches away. Her eyes were hard and cold under her slouch hat. Whatever it was that had made Joan snap like this, Lee couldn't help but snap back. They were both sporting the rarely seen GO AHEAD, I DARE YOU.

There had only been two occasions in their best friendship when they had faced off like this. Once in seventh grade, Joan had confessed to Lee that she had a crush on Django Flerk, and Lee had gone ahead and told J'dah Washington all about it. And just last month, Joan had made fun of Lee's stack of Big Brain books, calling them childish. Both times, the intensity of the anger between them had been swift and real, but it quickly faded, too.

This was no mere hurt-feelings argument. The whole world had narrowed to this little tunnel of disagreement between Lee and Joan.

Sam was furiously pretending to rebait the bent-nail fishing hooks.

It would be easy to give into Joan, Lee knew, but he was not going to. He'd thought he was simply enjoying the past, but Joan's sudden intensity made him realize that he wanted—*seriously* wanted—to stay here. What was there to go back to?

"No," Lee said, very quietly. "I do not want to go

back to the future. I like it here, and I'm staying here. And you should, too."

"You had better be kidding," she said rather harshly. "Our parents are probably half spazzed to death. We're one hundred and forty-eight years from home, and Chinese-hating butchers are looking for Mark Twain, who's that guy right there. You're cool with all that?"

The argument was on. Words flew around the deck of the *Paul Jones*. This was no logical debate, not even a heated argument. Joan and Lee were simply tossing words around. Spitting them.

"But you . . ." "Oh, no, you don't . . ." "I never thought . . ." "I always knew . . ." "You're so . . ." "You're such a . . ." "I don't believe a single . . ." "What the heck . . ."

Joan was headed to the future, that was the upshot of what she was saying, and what Lee was trying to get across was, "I don't care, go ahead."

At one point, Lee actually found himself shouting, "I know I'm shouting, I like to shout."

What stopped Lee's shouting was an even louder shout. It came from the ship next door.

"Sam Clemens!" the shouter shouted, "you owdacious puppy, I have never in my born days!"

This shout was like a shotgun blast.

On the deck of the next-door ship, stood two women, each holding real, live shotguns.

"Why, Misses Gr—" Sam began.

"Don't you 'Misses' us, you chucklehead," the other woman shouted. "Haven't you fed these children? Just listen to them."

Sam bowed and doffed an imaginary hat.

"I offer my humblest apology, Miss Greta," he said.

"Sorry don't milk the goat," Miss Greta said. "Now, y'all git on over here."

Miss Penelope scooched a gangplank across the space between the two ships, and silently and dutifully Joan and Lee and Sam crossed over to the deck of the *Darcy Cleaver.*

They continued to berate Sam, calling him a "nefarious coyote" and a "puddinhead." Apparently, last night, when the Misses Greta and Penelope had brought dinner to the *Paul Jones,* Sam had not conducted "proper introductions." The Misses Greta and Penelope were offended.

Then they shook hands with Lee and Joan, with extreme formality and big warm smiles. They curtsied, too. It surprised Lee that their emotions could morph from rage to civility in so short a time.

There was much that surprised Lee about these women. There were their shotguns, of course, but they also wore men's coats, blue jeans, and heavy workman's boots. They smoked hand-rolled cigarettes. Their gray hair was cut shorter than Sam's. In 2012 San Francisco, Lee knew, these women wouldn't be at all surprising. The woman who owned the Charlotte's Web bookstore in Lee's neighborhood, she dressed exactly like this and laughed as loud as a pirate and cursed like one, too. But in 1864, finding women dressed as men struck Lee as almost impossible.

Joan pulled her hat far down over her face and was staring at the deck. Lee saw she was truly afraid.

Sam reached over and pulled off Joan's hat.

"It's all right, Joan," he said. "Miss Penelope and Miss Greta are the best of people."

"Now, you possum-licker," Miss Greta said. "Let's get to vittals afore the sourdough gets cold and the crab gets warm."

The misses led them into their main cabin, above-decks, which was as pink and frilly as a tea shop. There a feast was laid out. Freshly toasted and buttered sourdough bread, "ship baked," bowls of chilled crab meat, and a sweating pitcher of lemonade.

For a few minutes, Lee and Joan did nothing but eat, grunting a few answers to the misses' questions.

One question in particular got Lee's attention.

"Now, precisely which future are you from?" Miss Penelope asked.

Lee froze.

Joan looked straight at Lee. OOPS.

They looked to Sam, who merely shrugged and went back to sucking the meat out of an orange crab claw.

"No, see—" Lee started, but Miss Penelope stared him into silence, though rather warmly.

"Fret not," she said. "Don't take no mathematician to figure you're one of us, the both of you."

"True that," Miss Greta said. She flipped her cigarette out the cabin's window. "We are your people. You'll come to recognize us, as we recognize you. Unstuckers have a certain air."

"I could tell 'bout these 'uns last night in the dark," Miss Penelope said.

With food oh-so importantly in his belly, Lee's brain was working again.

"So, Sam," he said, "is that why you live here? Because you're all unstuck?"

"Oh, hell no," Miss Greta said. "Miss Penelope and myself have been traveling the great unstuck for ages. This scoundrel"—she thumbed in Sam's direction—"why, he's a mewling wolf pup compared to us. Hee."

Without skipping a beat, Miss Penelope threaded

herself into the next sentence. "Though when he moved in a few months back, we knew, if he didn't."

"We remembered Sam when he first moved in last May," Miss Greta said. "We first met him in, what, '52, I think, a couple of years after we'd first come unstuck. We found him wandering the docks and took him in. Course Sam didn't remember us yet."

Joan and her math-logic brain hopped on this.

"So," she said, "you remembered Sam when you met him a few months ago because you had already met him in 1852. But a few months ago, Sam hadn't come unstuck for the first time. So he couldn't remember you yet."

"Oh, the first time's the most important," Miss Penelope said. "We couldn't tell him a few months ago. It don't do much good to tell someone who hasn't come unstuck yet that they will. Hard to sell a flying horse before it flies."

"Indeed," Sam said. "I recall that day well, I was—"

"Sam," Miss Greta said. "Hush up now. I believe our friends were talking to *us*." She turned to Lee. "He can be a most uncivilized brute. Now, which future is yours?"

Lee did most of the talking. He told the Misses Greta and Penelope about coming unstuck in the lighthouse, and everything he could about life in 2012. The misses seemed as unimpressed with the future as Sam had been.

"So," Lee wanted to know, "does this happen to everyone, coming unstuck? Is this some big adult secret our parents have been keeping from us?"

"Lordy, no," Miss Penelope said. "What a mess that would be, people coming unstuck all over the place."

"Why," Miss Greta said, "nothing would ever get done. People falling in and out of time. Preposterous."

"No," Miss Penelope said, "there's only a handful of us. We are your people. Fellow unstuckers."

"But why us?" Lee said.

This whole time, Joan was busy tracing on her forearm with her index finger. This was a "visualization" technique she used for the hardest algebra problems.

"Far as a body can know," Miss Greta said, "it's merely 'cause we're the type of people who are prone to it."

"May I?" Miss Penelope said, looking at Miss Greta.

"Do," Miss Greta said.

"Miss Greta and I, we've known each other since before we knew each other."

Miss Penelope took Miss Greta's hand and didn't let go.

"Growing up in high society Memphis, back in

Tennessee, as we did, we were our only and dearest friends. As we came into our majority, we found the world wanted us to live a certain way, and one way only. We were to wear silk dresses. We were to marry men others deemed appropriate for us. We were to live lives we had not designed for ourselves."

Miss Greta wiped a tear from her steel gray eyes. Miss Penelope tightened her grasp on her friend's hand and continued.

"Not liking the shapes of our futures, we departed our families and our corsets and our childhood Memphis, and we set out west, always west. In 1835. We saw a great many things on our journeys, but from town to town and city to city, we never did find a place that felt like *our* home. It was luck—pure chance—that brought us to San Francisco in the wake of the Gold Rush. It was during our first week here, we came unstuck, out by where Fort Point now stands. We continued unstuck for a while, but when we returned to our own time, we knew San Francisco was home. We've lived here fourteen years now."

Miss Greta and Miss Penelope traded a tender LOOK. SWEET.

Joan sat forward.

"Is it only in San Francisco?" she said. "Do people only come unstuck at Fort Point?"

"Oh, no," Miss Greta said. She let go of Miss Penelope's hand and wiped her eyes clear. "There are other places we've heard about. But San Francisco's a good one. Very popular that way. People come here to find their futures. You can be who you want to be here. Keep a remember on that."

Something shifted in Lee's brain, a fresh connection made. That's why he'd been unhappy with the future he saw the morning of the field trip. He wasn't going to be who he wanted to be. Other people had made huge decisions on his behalf. He knew exactly what the misses were talking about.

Joan was tracing on her arm again, then she erased everything.

"But why?" she said. "Why does it even happen? Unstuck. It doesn't make sense." Joan looked at Lee like everything was his fault somehow.

"Asking that is like arguing with a stone, dearie," Miss Penelope said. "You're here, aren't you? You can ask questions of the stone all day, but it's still a stone."

"Fine," Joan said. "But how does it work? How do we come unstuck again? Get back to our own time?"

"Oh," Miss Greta said. "That's easy. You go forward. That's how to come unstuck again."

"Forward?" Lee said. "Which way is forward?" He was confused again.

"Every step is forward," Miss Greta said. "Whether you're in the past, present, or future, every step takes you forward. No denying that. It's all about moving, going *towards* something."

"Sittin' 'round fishin' with this lunk." Miss Penelope thumbed at Sam. "That won't help none. It's why you two were fighting so fierce just now. You, Joan, you want to be in the future; Lee here wants to stay in the past. But until you do decide to make some kind of move, well, you'll be fishing forever."

"So you can control it?" Joan said. "The unstuck?"

"Of a fashion," Miss Greta said. "But be careful. Time has a mind of its own."

"How do we make a move?" Lee said. "Which way? Towards what?"

"Don't much matter," Miss Penelope said. "Take a step. You may not know where you'll end up, but you won't be here. Dangerous or not, unknown or not: go."

And just like that, the misses' tone reversed again. Lee knew lunch was over.

"Consarn it, Sam Clemens," Miss Greta said, "or Mr. Mark Twain—oh, la-di-da—or whoever you will be. You get these young 'uns out of here. Hear? We've done our civil duty, but a beautiful day awaits us. Look at this weather. We shall not waste one day. I suggest you all do the same."

Miss Greta stood and began clearing the plates and cups. Miss Penelope joined her.

"We bid you farewell," Miss Greta said. "For the moment. Soon again, we hope. Now git."

Lee could think more clearly about his argument with Joan. She did have a point, he saw. They couldn't stay in 1864 forever. As soon as they were back on the *Paul Jones*, Lee took Joan by the elbow and turned her to face him.

"You're right," Lee said to her. "We should go back to the future. I'm sorry we fought. Let's go forward, like they said. I'm sorry." FOR REALS.

"I'm sorry, too," Joan said. I MEAN IT. "And you're right, Lee. It won't kill us to stay a little longer. We still need some kind of plan. And we're safe here with Sam. I could use a bath, anyway. I feel so gnarly."

"A bath?" Sam said. "Oh, you children of the future. What have they done to you? Are you certain? It takes a good while to rustle up a proper bath."

"Please, Sam. It's a girl thing."

"Master Lee?"

"I'm cool," Lee said. "I don't need no stinkin' bath."

Sam grinned. "I was just about to lose my faith in all children. Follow me, Miss Joan. Gettin' scrubbed's a lot of work."

Sam and Joan moved to the stern to begin what he

called the "laborious" task of drawing a bath. Lee went forward to check the fishing lines. They'd actually caught some kind of fish. A flounder? Lee unhooked it and tossed it back into the bay.

Yes, he was ready to go back into the future. Just not *all* the way back. He had a big idea.

TEN

The Problem with Baths –
Time Is a River – "Cast Off!" –
Back in the Current –
An Herbal Remedy

Enough with the past already. Joan had had it up to here with the good old days. She had been able to take a bath and was now clean—sort of—but it took so much work.

Sam found a messenger to fetch the water cart, then endless heavy buckets were hauled up on deck with painful ropes, one bucket at a time. The galley's cook stove was stoked and lit and the water heated—this took hours—then the water was lowered into the hold, bucket by bucket, and finally the captain's tin tub was filled. But the tub was only three feet long, the soap smelled like poison and felt like sandpaper, and the water was robbed of all heat in about a minute. The only towel was a small square of burlap. How could people live in 1864?

So by the time she dressed again, Joan was ready to skip the past entirely. In fact, she was so anxious to get back to the future, she thought she'd go a little beyond where she and Lee had started from. Why go back to deal with that crazy divorce, and being separated from Lee, and tests and high school, and tests and college. No, Joan thought she'd fly ahead to a time when she'd have her own apartment and a cool car and a fun job, when life was easy and all you had to do was turn the faucet's handle and hot steaming water poured over you. And she'd stay there.

When she went up on deck, the sun was already setting, another warm, calm evening. Lee and Sam were ensconced in the pilothouse. Sam listened intently, while Lee sketched something in a notebook with a goose quill pen.

"'S'up, my peeps?" Joan said.

"'S'up, my peep?" Sam said. He was really good at picking up slang, even if he didn't know what he was saying.

"Working on a plan," Lee said. "We're here, see, and we need to get to the fort, but in between, there's all this San Francisco. And, you know, butchers and stuff."

Lee pointed to some blotches and smears and squiggles. "We dress up as Indians and build a canoe. Then we paddle to the fort and demand a parlay with the colonel. When we've gained his trust—"

Sam put up a hand to stop Lee, and a good thing, too, or Joan would have done it.

"A doozy of a plan," Sam said. "But the thing is, it takes about a year to make a proper canoe. And while I applaud your, uh, inventiveness, perhaps we might streamline your idea."

Lee seemed quite embarrassed. "Okay," he said, "we build a submarine."

Sam laughed. Joan had to, too.

"But really," Lee said, "how do we get back?"

Joan leaped in.

"We go forward, right?" she said, looking to Sam. "Make a move. That's what the misses said. Go forward. *Want* to get back."

"Sam," Lee said, "tell us how you got restuck."

Sam moved to the brass ship's wheel and stared far away. He pulled out his pipe.

"Not in here," Joan said. "You'll kill us."

Sam grumbled and put his pipe back in his pocket. "As I told you before," he said, "I grew up on the banks of the great river, which is the Mississippi, which is the only river, the world's river."

"Is this really the best time for a colorful childhood anecdote?" Joan wanted to punch Sam a little, a friendly get-on-with-it punch.

"I declare," he said, turning on her. "People ask questions as if they want you to answer, then find themselves unable to hear the true answer because it's not the one they wanted."

Lee looked at Joan. DEEP BREATH.

"Asides," Sam said, "if I'm ever to be this Mark Twain fellow, this great American storyteller, I might as well get some practice."

Joan registered the sneer of Sam's lips when he said "Twain."

He swung the ship's wheel sharply.

"As a boy, I spent as much time on the river as allowed—rafts, canoes, sometimes nothing more than a tree branch. I vowed that one day I would become that most exalted creature, a riverboat pilot. So I set my mind to it, and eventually became one, and up and down the river, again and again, that was my life, and all I ever wanted of it."

Joan was tapping her foot. She made herself stop.

"Time is a river," Sam said, "in answer to your question. The two share so much in common, a study of one may assist our study of the other."

Joan was listening now.

"I knew that river," Sam said, "as well as any pilot who ever charged it. And yet I hardly knew that river at all. A river is impossible to reckon. Hardly worth the trouble to make a map of. Every journey down the river, the river changes. Cliffs rise and fall. Bends straighten out; whole new bends appear. What had been on your last trip a narrow channel you could skip a stone across might suddenly be a mile-wide crossing. The river is alive, and like all living things, it constantly changes."

Sam spun the wheel of the *Paul Jones*.

"You never know what's around the next bend. It could be a long stretch of deep, swift current or a nasty shallows with treacherous sandbars. And sometimes what you think is the river 'cause it's so wide, is actually just another channel around the far side of a huge island you've never seen before. But you don't know you're in that channel until you join up with the main river again. Coming unstuck, it seems to me, is sort of like that. A diversion, if you will, a peeling away from the main current."

Joan could see this, the river, with its big island, she and Lee separated from the main stream. She wasn't sure it made sense, in a science-fact kind of way, but she could see it, feel it.

"Permit me a digression, please," Sam said. "It is in my nature to do so. The main current is where we all strive to be, but do not overlook these side-excursions. Often such side-excursions are the life of our life-voyage."

This Joan understood clearly. Where she and Lee were now was a diverted channel, a side-excursion. It was important, somehow, to be here, away from the main. For a while at least. Even if it felt strange. She felt all this as a fact.

"That must be why we came unstuck," she said. "The lesson Lee and I are supposed to learn."

Sam stared her down. "Hang lessons," he said. "Blast the moral a story's supposed to bear. Lessons ruin a good adventure."

Joan opened her mouth to speak. Sam stopped her, glaring.

"Patience," he said. "Back to my story. When I came unstuck and saw I might one day be that Twain fellow, it give me a deep shiver. Everyone said this Twain was a great writer, but how could I ever be that? So I stayed unstuck in time, in that side channel. I was so fearful of my future, I got myself mired in an eddy."

"Who's Eddie?" Lee asked.

Joan elbowed him.

"An eddy," Sam said, "is a pocket in the river, usually along the banks, where water circles in on itself and stops flowing. You can sit and stew there, for hours, days, watching all the other ships go by. I got stuck in such an eddy, afraid of who I might be, afraid I couldn't do what was needed. It was only when I decided to stop being afraid and start trying to be Twain, be that writer I always wanted to be, that I got back to the river and its constant tug forward."

"Like us," Joan said. "Me and Lee, we're in kind of an eddy right now."

"But how do we get out of the eddy?" Lee asked.

"First rule of the river pilot," Sam said. "Full steam ahead, open all the valves. Like the misses said. Make a move. You have to run the river. If you let the river carry you, you'll get carried away. Maintain power, you maintain control. Even in a rapids."

Lee sat up at this, though he looked a little pale. "There's rapids in time, too?" he asked.

"My, yes," Sam said. "We call it a tumble. Every once in a while, with no warning, you find yourself careering from time to time, too quickly to count."

"That doesn't sound so good," Lee said. Lee didn't look so good.

Joan was interested in the idea of time rapids, a

tumble, but she was more interested in getting started again.

"So we just go," Joan said. "Make a move."

"Put the oar in the water," Sam said, "and row. The only way I know of."

"Which means what?" Lee said. "I mean, yadda, yadda, yadda, river and eddy and rapids and all, I get it. But where do we go? *Actually*? You know, like in reality?"

"There was something to your plan, Lee," Sam said. "Fort Point's as good a place as any. A boat's too dangerous at night, though. We'll have to hoof it through town. It'll be dark. We should be safe."

"But the Chinese Menace? The butchers? Joan? It's too dangerous." Lee was standing up now, his fists balled.

"I can do it," Joan said. "I'll take the chance."

"Are you both ready? To head back to your futures?" Sam asked. "At least in that direction."

"Absolutely," Joan said. Though she didn't say anything about *which* future she had in mind.

"Me, too," Lee said, "I want to go back. I really do."

Joan and Lee looked at each other, and the LOOK they shared was NO LOOK, not a single piece of information shared. Joan knew she was hiding something from Lee, but what was Lee hiding from her?

"Cast off," Sam said. "Throw off the bowlines. Set sail."

Out the pilothouse window, directly over the ship's bow, the first bright star of the evening showed itself.

At first the gaslight and carriages and trains and crowds of the Market Street night drew panic into Joan. She felt exposed, and Sam hadn't helped, either. Lee had been after Sam to hire a carriage to take them to Fort Point, but Sam thought it dangerous. The Kearny Street butchers, he told them, were Irish, and had many Irish friends among the city's carriage drivers.

But as they moved into the city, Joan felt more at ease. Whether it was 1864 or not, San Francisco was a big city. Who could ever find them here? Still, she kept her slouch hat pulled over her face.

With Sam and Lee on either side of her, they headed west on Market, towards Fort Point. The whole time Lee and Sam were concocting various plans to get back into the lighthouse, though none of them sounded plausible. Lee's most daring plan involved a catapult. Joan had no idea, really, what was going to happen at Fort Point; it just felt good to be out of the eddy.

All along Market, people were selling things. Shovels

and chickens and cheap sparkly jewelry from store-fronts where, Joan knew, others would be selling souvenir ashtrays and sweatshirts and cheap sparkly jewelry in 2012.

At one corner, two men, who a sign declared THE KING AND THE DUKE, were selling bottles of pills guaranteed, The King said, to enhance one's vocabulary and eloquence. When The Duke, obviously playing the shill, a mumbling and bumbling fool, took one of these pills, he immediately began to spout lines from Shakespeare—Joan recognized *Romeo and Juliet*.

At another corner, a man Sam called Oofty Goofty allowed customers to punch him in the stomach for a nickel each. The line here was very long.

In front of the Argonaut Opera House, a boisterous crowd had gathered, and Sam allowed them to stop. Joan felt safe in the crowd.

There stood a bearded man in a fancy military uniform with spangles of gold all over it. He wore a plumed hat that made him look like the commanding general of a fairy-tale army. He was distributing small scrolls of paper to those who approached him, in exchange for which he was given coins. Two dogs—a large black-and-white one and a smaller golden mutt—sat on either side of the general like palace guards.

"Norton the First," Sam told them. "Emperor of the

United States and Protector of all Mexico. And his faithful companions Bummer and Lazarus."

Emperor Norton? Who didn't know about him? Joan had done a report, of course. Norton had declared himself ruler of the continent, and the people of San Francisco had let him act as if he were their emperor. Norton was only one in a long line of crazy people the city called its own.

"We may need his protection," Sam said. He approached the emperor with a deep bow.

"How may the emperor aid his faithful citizens?"

Sam swept his hand towards Joan and Lee.

"We seek safe passage to a strange land," Sam said. "We implore your highness for his royal decree. All respect the wishes of Norton the First. Will you help us, my liege?"

"For a nickel, I will," the emperor intoned. The crowd laughed.

Sam offered up a nickel with great ceremony. The emperor put it in his pocket. He adjusted his hat.

"I hereby decree," he boomed, "that these faithful citizens be granted fair winds and safe harbors."

The emperor handed a scroll to Joan and smiled graciously upon her. She unfurled it, but it was blank. Sam moved forward to speak to the emperor privately.

Lee banged Joan in the ribs with his elbow.

"Over there," he whispered. "Is that him?"

On the far side of the crowd was the stranger in black, the one Joan had seen, and Lee, too, the one who had evaporated before their eyes. He was moving towards them, waving. A chill froze Joan. Was he one of the butchers?

Great big scary OMGs swept over their faces.

Then the stranger simply evaporated again—pfft. But Joan was taking no chances. She grabbed Sam's coat and pulled him away from the emperor, and Lee was turning him around. Time to motor.

Bam. Right into a great big scary looking guy. One who did not evaporate.

"Well, well," this un-evaporating man said. "Mr. Mark Twain, I do declare. How fortunate to run into you on this fine evening. My friends and I have been looking for you. Seems you've been telling a story we're not so fond of."

Joan looked up at Sam. His face was stony, unmoving, but she saw enough in it to know who this was. One of the butchers.

Joan tried to look down and away, to keep her face hidden, but the great big scary guy bent down and looked under her hat. He pulled it off her head.

"What have we here?" the man said. "A girl, not a boy. And a Chinese girl, too. My, my, Mr. Twain. I do believe my friends will be most interested in meeting your companion."

The man grabbed Joan by the arm, but Lee pulled her away, and Sam shoved the great big scary guy down to the ground, into the crowd around the emperor. The crowd, laughing, surrounded the man. Sam and Lee, and most especially Joan, took off.

"Vamoose," Sam said. "Chinatown. We've a friend there. Run."

And they were off, running north now. Joan didn't dare look behind her. The feel of that man's hand on her arm still burned.

The Chinatown Joan knew was festooned with strings of paper lanterns and fluorescent signs and had grocers whose produce spilled out onto the sidewalks and lots of tacky tourist shops and a billion restaurants. A giant ornamental dragon-decorated arch welcomed visitors from around the world.

In this Chinatown, all that welcomed them was darkness.

This Chinatown was crowded, too, but that was the end of the comparison. The streets were unpaved, muddy, as narrow as streets could be. No banners, no lanterns.

Nothing bright at all. The shops and the apartments above them were wooden stick figure buildings, slanted and rickety.

But the biggest difference was that there were no families in this Chinatown. Joan saw it in a glance. Her Chinatown was nothing but families, from the tiniest children to the oldest grandparents. Every Sunday, Joan's family went to Chinatown for dim sum at Baba's favorite restaurant, the Jade Flower. Oh, the pork buns, the shrimp buns, the hundred varieties of buns, all chosen from carts wheeled past the table. The crowded, noisy table; the crowded, noisy, delicious restaurant. The family together.

This Chinatown, where she stood now, was a shadow parade of shadow-faced men all dressed in shadows. The men seemed intolerably lonely. Joan missed dim sum Sundays. She missed Baba. Missed her family and the lights and crowds of her Chinatown.

The shadow men cleared a path for the three strangers.

They stopped at a dark corner, looked back. So far, so good.

"It's not much farther," Sam said. "We can hide with Gim for a while. Gather ourselves. We'll cut through here. Shortcuts are always exciting."

Hiding, Joan thought. She liked that idea.

Sam ducked into a narrow alley, and Joan and Lee scooted in after him. There were lots of narrow alleys in Chinatown, but Joan had never bothered to follow one, and she was surprised to find a large sunken court-yard behind the crowded-together shops. Laundry-strewn balconies hung over the courtyard. A dead end? Ooh, not a good expression.

They stepped into the courtyard, but Joan turned at a scraping sound from the alley. Over Lee's shoul-der, she saw the silhouette of a man moving towards them.

"Sam," she whispered. She tugged on his coat, and when he turned, he saw the man, too, and he swore.

The man stopped in the alley. He raised a hand—almost as if he were waving, Joan thought—and called, "Sam, Sam, stop, stop."

"Yonder!" Sam yelled, and he pushed Lee and Joan across the courtyard, and they were running, and then they were in another narrow alley, and they were run-ning faster.

They came out on a dark but crowded shopping street, weaving through crowds of shadow men. They were running hard, but Joan found the courage to look behind her. No one was chasing them. She looked at Lee. PHEW.

Then that little pocket of safety collapsed. From

behind them, from another direction, Joan heard hard-soled footfalls galloping. She kept her eye on Sam, kept her ears peeled for Lee, who was right behind her.

"Stop! Twain!" someone was yelling. "Stop now, Twain! We've got you."

Sam skidded around a corner like a cartoon cat, and Joan and Lee skidded after. The footfalls drew closer.

Joan was a terrific runner—she actually loved it—and would have no trouble keeping up with Sam's full-tilt sprint. But Lee. When it came to running, well, let's just say, running was not Lee's thing.

"Gotcha!" the stranger cried, and for a second the voice was really close to Joan. Then she heard the deep thud of a body being slammed into a wall, and then Lee's voice, choked, calling, "Help!"

Joan stopped on a dime.

The stranger had pinned Lee to the wall, his arm shoved into his throat. It was the big scary guy from Market Street, and he was yelling, "Twain! I've got one of your little friends!"

The crowds of shadow men glided by.

"Sam!" Joan yelled, and she was impressed with what an awful noise she made. She didn't know she had it in her—it was a horror-movie scream.

She froze for a minute, looking directly into the face of the big scary guy. He wore a crooked, ugly smile, and

Joan knew the smile was for her. She could tell the man was simply toying with Lee; it was Joan he wanted to hurt. There was no doubt he would hurt her.

But Lee.

Joan was on the man in an instant, kicking him and punching him and pushing him and trying to get Lee free. There was no thought involved in this. She just did it. Had to. She whaled on him.

Sam flew in from out of nowhere, traveling at full speed, and knocked into the stranger—there was a blur of sound and motion and bodies colliding, then the stranger was flat on his back and gasping for air.

They were off again, running in the middle of the street now. Joan pushed Lee ahead of her—she'd make him keep up—and Lee was moving pretty fast, the soldier's backpack bumping along.

Just before they turned the next corner, Joan hazarded another glance behind her. The big scary guy was still on his back, not looking so scary anymore.

Then oomph, oomph. Sam had stopped short, and Lee bumped into him, and Joan bumped into Lee.

Five men stood in a line that blocked the street. There was no question. Butchers. Each of them wore a blood-stained apron and held a cleaver.

Sam reached for his derringer, but then he seemed to reconsider the rash move he was about to make—could you shoot five men with one tiny pistol? Sam spread his arms wide, keeping Lee and Joan behind him.

"Twain," one of the men yelled, "you can write but you can't hide."

All of the men laughed.

"Evening to you," Sam said. And he tipped his hat. "I'd call you gentlemen, but I don't know you well enough for that intimacy."

"We've got a little lesson we'd like to teach you," the man said very quietly. Joan could not see his face. "And for your little Chinese friend, too."

The butchers were several shop fronts down the block, but they seemed much closer. Otherwise, the street was now empty.

Sam put his hands behind his back. He waved his fingers furiously for a moment, trying to get Joan and Lee's attention. Then he held one fist steady. Joan and Lee looked at each other. ON THREE.

"Now, now, my confused fellows," Sam said to the butchers. He held out one finger. "It's always a delight to run into the masters of meat." Two fingers. "I was just thinking about a nice bowl of tripe, and here you are." Three fingers.

"However . . ."

Sam closed his fist, and the three of them turned in

unison and beat it back around the corner they'd come from.

The big scary guy was just now getting to his feet when Lee plowed into his shoulder and sent him sprawling again. Wow, look at Lee go.

Behind them, the voices of the butchers—loud, angry. No words, just sound.

Sam pushed them into and down another alley, and instantly they were out of that alley on another shopping street. Sam drew them to a stop and rather rudely shoved them into a shop's open door. He pulled them down behind the front counter and squished them to the floor.

A startled shopkeeper stood next to them. He was an elderly Chinese man dressed in a gown of gorgeous blue silk embroidered all over with gold thread.

"Ah, Sam," he said, "always a pleasure."

The shopkeeper wore an amused smile. Sam put a finger to his lips, then put his hands together in a pitiful prayer. The shopkeeper nodded, closed his face, and returned to his task.

Joan couldn't see what the man was doing, but she recognized the shop, at least the kind of shop. Behind the counter were tall rows of wooden drawers, and on other shelves there were glass jars filled with roots and leaves and mushrooms. This was an herbalist. There was still a shop very much like this in Chinatown today—well, in 2012. She'd gone to the herbalist a couple of times with her father. Whenever his stomach was upset, he made a tea from roots he purchased there. The tea smelled awful.

In the next instant, the front of the store was filled with heat and noise. The butchers.

"Where are they?" the leader called. "Which way did they go?"

"Me no unna'tan'," the shopkeeper said. "You wan' herb, root?" He held up a pile of shavings.

"Rotten China Man," the leader said, and the knot of butchers backed out of the shop.

Joan watched the shopkeeper's face as he watched the men moving down the street.

"Follow me," the shopkeeper said as if talking to himself.

He disappeared behind a short curtain, and the three of them crawled along the floor of the shop. The back room smelled of rotting leaves. They stood now, and Lee hugged Joan as he'd never hugged her.

"Thank you, Gim," Sam said, and he and the shop-keeper shook hands. "These are my friends, Joan and Lee. I wish we had time for pleasantries, but we should get out of here before those hooligans return."

"Not to worry," Gim said. "But promise me the next time you'll stay for a pipe. It's been too long, Sam. This way."

Gim ushered them out a rear door to yet another narrow alley. "Follow this down the hill. It'll take you to the waterfront. Find a carriage, something fancy. No one will look for a reporter in a landau."

Joan tugged on Sam's sleeve. "A carriage? Sam, you said that could be dangerous."

Sam's face was put on pause for a second. "That's true," he said, "but the waterfront can be even more dangerous this time of night. We'll have to take our chances. Gim's right."

Oh, swell, Joan thought. More danger.

The shopkeeper handed Sam some coins, then turned his attention to Joan.

"Keep your hat down," he said to her.

"*Sheh-sheh*," Joan said

"You're welcome," he said. "*Yat lou ping on.*"

Her baba often used the same phrase—peace and safety on the road.

It was near total darkness in this alley and very steep and muddy, too, but there were some wooden planks that acted as a walkway and kept them above the mud. Joan used the narrow walls to keep her balance.

This was her dream. The one she'd had before

coming unstuck in the lighthouse at Fort Point. The narrow walkway, the mud, the tight alley. In that dream when she slipped off the walkway, that's when she'd come unstuck.

She didn't know if it would happen again; she didn't know if she wanted it to happen again. If she came unstuck, *when* would she be? Would she be at home? Would she land in the future she desired or in some other dangerous past?

One of the boards tilted suddenly, and she splashed in the mud.

"Lee?" Joan called into the darkness.

ELEVEN

The Near Future –
A Surprise Party – Pirates –
Sailing, Sailing – A Short Trip

This was the most scared Lee had ever been.

No, wait a minute, that wasn't true at all.

He checked himself: nope, not scared. He was supposed to be scared, but he wasn't. He'd been smashed up against a wall by that big ugly goon, and butchers with cleavers had chased them down the street. The only plan now was the old herbalist's—go down a dark, narrow alley. I mean, seriously. This was the phrase that kept popping into his head: *I mean, seriously.*

But Lee was calm, clear-headed, solid. And at the same time, a little thrilled. Was this feeling, he wondered, what people meant when they said "in shock"?

Hardly mattered; he liked it. He knew that Joan had a lot to do with how he was feeling.

Lee would be a liar if he said he wasn't scared when that goon plastered him against the wall in Chinatown. Along with a fiery flush of fear, he'd had two thoughts at that moment: First, he kind of wished he'd brought along a second pair of pants, and second, this wasn't at all how he'd pictured his own death. But Joan, Joan wheeled and, without a single hesitation, threw herself on the big scary guy. She'd shown no fear at all, and Lee knew she'd risked her own safety because it was he, Lee, who was in trouble. She'd thought nothing of herself at that moment. After that, how could he be scared? It was no rational decision to stop being scared; it just happened, blossomed in his heart.

Near the end of the dark alley, he heard Joan slip off the narrow walkway, then the fear in her voice when she called out for him. He could tell she didn't know where she was for a minute, was afraid she might have come unstuck in time again. It was easy to reach out, find her, squeeze her arm and hold her hand, tell her everything was okay, and keep her moving.

The alley dumped Sam and Joan and Lee on the waterfront, where an armada of ships blocked the view of the bay. Even though it was past dark, many of the ships were still being loaded and unloaded. Huddles of men roamed through the half gloom of the gaslight's green glow. Were these other gangs? With other weapons? Cleavers? Swords, pistols? Was there anywhere in San Francisco that wasn't dangerous? Didn't matter. Lee was too thrilled and grateful to be frightened.

Sam hailed a passing carriage and bundled them into it. The driver was hesitant to pick up this scruffy threesome, until Sam flashed his hundred-dollar gold coin.

"South Park ships," Sam called to the driver.

Lee looked over at Joan. They gave each other THE EYEBROW. Back to the *Paul Jones*?

"What about Fort Point?" Lee said. "We're going there, remember?"

"A mite dangerous. I believe a retreat might be in order." Sam kept his eyes trained on the docks. "We'll regroup there, start again in the morning. Who knows where the butchers might be right now."

Joan looked at Lee. THE DOUBLE EYEBROW. Joan started to speak, but Lee had this one covered.

"No way," Lee said. "We're not going back to the *Paul Jones*. 'Cast off' and all that. Remember? You said."

Lee *had* wanted to stay in the past, but Joan had rightly convinced him otherwise. They couldn't stay here in 1864. They needed to get back to the future. Maybe not as far back as Joan imagined, but pretty close. Maybe to the year when Lee was eight. The time in his family's life that Lee remembered best. They went on two vacations that year, one to the Santa Cruz Beach Boardwalk and one—oh, my God—to Disneyland. His birthday was a great day in the park, Halloween on Belvedere Street had been a blast—he was Admiral Sharkey from *Starcruiser Omega*, a costume his mom made herself, most excellently. And their Christmas tree that year was the biggest one ever. They'd had to cut a foot off the top to squeeze it into the house. Even back then, when he was just a little kid, he knew it was a great year; even school had been fun, with Mrs. Meadows. And his best friendship with Joan was still ahead of him. He and his parents had talked and laughed a lot that year. Since then there hadn't been as much laughing. He hated the new silence that filled his house these days.

When Lee heard Misses Greta and Penelope talking about going forward, about *wanting* to get back, he got a big idea. They'd only go to the near future, when he was eight, and then he'd do something. Here his plan got vague, but if he could change the past, maybe he could make his future better. He'd think of some way to make his parents happy again. You could do that in time-travel novels, right? Change the past, change the future.

He hadn't told Joan about his idea yet. He was pretty sure she'd try to talk him out of it. It *did* sound crazy.

But crazy or not, he was going to give it a whirl, and no way was he going to let Sam make them retreat to the *Paul Jones*. Keep going forward.

Lee had spaced out of the conversation in the carriage. When he returned, Joan and Sam were squabbling.

"Sam, you said—"

"Joan, you have to understand—"

"It doesn't make sense to—"

"But that's not the point—"

"Sailing," Lee said, but he said it too quietly, and it got swallowed up.

"Sailing!" Lee bellowed.

Everyone shut up. Even the jangling of the carriage was stilled.

Sam and Joan shared a LOOK. SHUT UP. Not as in, "Be quiet," but as in, "I don't believe you just said that!"

"Sailing?" Joan asked.

"Sam's sailboat," Lee said. "We can sail around to Fort Point, skip the city altogether. It's dark."

Joan looked at Lee with genuine admiration. Lee was glad it was dark in the carriage. He was pretty sure he was blushing.

"Mighty risky," Sam said. "Sailing at night."

"Sam," Lee said, and in that one word was all the accusation and challenge he could muster.

"Really, Sam," Joan said. "Not very Mark Twain of you. He didn't write all those books by playing it safe."

Sam roared with laughter.

"Yeah," Lee said, "cast off, batten the hatches, enjibben the mainsail, and other nautical stuff. Go forward."

Sam's laughter ebbed. He wiped his eyes. "Enjibben the mainsail, indeed, Master Lee. Sailing, it is. But it carries danger, you know?"

Lee and Joan: PLEASE. As in, "You don't have to tell us."

"Cast off," Sam said.

The carriage bounced along at a good clip, but it bounced more than it clipped. Lee was certain the automobile had been a less-than-awesome invention, as much damage as it had caused the planet, but he found a new appreciation for the shock absorber. His butt was going to hurt tomorrow—that was certain.

The driver dropped them off at the east end of the Street of Ships. Only the lowest of the low lived in these ships, and he wasn't going to risk his "exquisite" carriage. Not even for a passenger with a hundred-dollar gold coin. He expected, he said, that Sam would pay him on the morrow, when he changed that coin, as Sam swore he would.

They crept along the ships' hulls, only a few of which showed any lights. It was late, Lee knew. A gibbous moon, waning, was nearly at its zenith. Close to midnight.

As the *Paul Jones* came into view, Sam shushed them. Trouble.

"We've got company," he said in a breathless whisper. "Looks as if poor Smiggy has been 'persuaded' to reveal our whereabouts."

Sam pointed to the windows of the captain's quarters. A faint glow spilled from it. A murmur of voices. Then "B'wah!"—a big laugh.

They glided below the starboard porthole. Sam made some strange and, to be totally honest, incomprehensible hand signs. Still, Lee got the picture. He was to peek in, see what was what. Recon.

Sam linked his fingers together to make a boost step, and without thinking, Lee stepped into Sam's hands.

The porthole window was filthy, smudged and greasy and flecked with bits of dirt and sand. But that mess didn't stop Lee from recognizing the scene in the captain's quarters. The butchers and their cleavers.

They sat around the captain's table, looking quite restless, pacing the cabin and knocking things over. The head butcher was using his cleaver to cut notches into the captain's table. He'd thwack the cleaver into the edge of the table, then thwack next to that mark, at an angle, and pull out a chip of wood. Even in his idleness, the butcher was violent.

He raised his cleaver high and, almost rising from his chair, slammed it into the table.

"Enough," the head butcher said. "He's not coming back."

Lee was frantically waving his left hand—get me down, get me down.

"It's them," Lee said. "And they're pretty mad. I think they're getting ready to leave." Lee was, all at once, whispering, miming, pleading, urging, begging.

Sam crouched again. Lee and Joan crouched, too. Sam led them towards the bow, down to the bay's shore, to the small sailboat. Noises were erupting from the *Paul Jones*—shouts, breaking glass, wood cracked open. Chaos.

Lee tossed the backpack into the sailboat, then he and Joan stepped in. Sam pushed off and hopped in, and they glided into the silent bay.

Hauling a rope, Sam raised the boat's mast to its full height and unfurled the sail.

The night was rocked by a shattering explosion, and in the next sweep of time, orange and yellow flames burst from the hold of the *Paul Jones*, followed by a gaggle of banshee-mad, cleaver-totin' butchers.

Before he had the chance to realize he was giving

away their position, Lee yelled out, "Sam!" and was pointing to the deck of the ship, where the butchers now stood.

"Twain!" the master butcher screamed.

The sailboat was only a few yards from shore, in shallow water, and Lee knew that the butchers could be on them in a few strides. The butchers, however, hadn't yet realized this and stood at the bow of the *Paul Jones*, looking like amateur pirates, Lee thought, weekend pirates. But Lee also knew they were dangerous.

Sam pulled out his derringer and cocked the hammer. But he wasn't aiming at the butchers. He unloaded a single round over the pilothouse of the *Darcy Cleaver*.

Lee inhaled sharply.

"Miss Greta!" Sam yelled. "Miss Penelope!"

The Misses Greta and Penelope, in frilly nightgowns and caps, popped up on their foredeck. They carried their shotguns, and those shotguns were aimed steadfastly at the butchers.

There was the sound of several cleavers hitting the deck.

"Miss Greta, Miss Penelope," Sam said, and he tipped his hat. "Evenin'. Sorry to disturb you."

"Not at all, Sam," Miss Greta said. "We're accustomed to saving your worthless hide."

Miss Penelope emptied two thunderous rounds of

shot out over the water, and both women began to yell, "Fire, fire, fire!" In a heartbeat, the Street of Ships was a hive of ringing bells and other clamorous activity.

Lee was pretty sure each and every one of the butchers wanted to jump ship, but the shotguns of Miss Greta and Miss Penelope persuaded them to remain.

While the flames from the *Paul Jones* licked into the night sky, Sam unfurled and hoisted the sail, and a soft southerly breeze caught and inflated it. The boat jerked once, then set off gliding over the black water.

Lee stared forlornly after the *Paul Jones*.

The waning moon offered enough light to enchant the night. The bay was black but visible. It was perfectly quiet out here, and Lee was happy with that.

They emerged from their sheltered cove into the open bay, and a stiff wind caught the sail. It felt to Lee as if a hand was pushing the boat from behind.

Up ahead was the black silhouette of Yerba Buena Island, partway between San Francisco and Oakland. Where the Bay Bridge and the man-made Treasure Island was supposed to be.

As the boat came even with the southern tip of Yerba Buena Island, a sharp hissing noise filled the air. But before Lee could turn, three sleek sails hove into view on their starboard. The three boats were longer and thinner than Sam's old clunker, and their sails were enormous. The boats rode low in the water, the sails tipped so far over they etched the surface of the bay. One dark shape manned each tiller.

In half a second, the sleek boats swished past them, cutting towards the northern tip of the island.

"Oyster pirates," Sam said. The quiet was broken for the first time since leaving the *Paul Jones*. "Out here every night. Thrilling, eh? And if I'm not mistaken . . ." Sam looked over his shoulder. "Yep," he said. "There's the harbor patrol."

Far behind, a small steamer chugged along, its black trail of smoke rising lazily into the star-strewn night. Three pinpoints of light—one green, one white, one red—marked the ship's progress. Lee knew this ship would never catch the oyster pirates.

Sam tacked away from Yerba Buena, riding closer to the anchored ships along what would one day be called the Embarcadero.

Joan and Lee looked at each other, gave each other THE NOD, and the quiet of the night sail captured them.

When they rounded the northern tip of San Francisco and headed west towards the Golden Gate, the currents grew swifter, more powerful. Swells rose; white caps broke around them. Fast going but tougher.

Sam kept them occupied by pointing out landmarks—even in danger, he had stories to tell. There was Alcatraz and its big guns and, behind it, the lurking shadow of Angel Island. From the shore, Meiggs' Wharf stuck out into the bay and, just past it, the enormous smokestack of the Pioneer Woolen Mills. Lee wasn't certain, but this might be the place where one day Fisherman's Wharf and Ghirardelli Square would stand. It had to be.

Now they were past inhabited San Francisco and headed along Crissy Field, or whatever it was called now, where nothing but a few low buildings smudged the shore. Ahead, the lighthouse of Fort Point called them to it.

Lee found it odd to see the Golden Gate without its bridge; the gap between San Francisco and Marin seemed infinitely more vast this way. The bridge, Lee realized, didn't just connect the two shores, it changed the way he saw the world around the bridge.

Sam pulled the tiller hard to, and the boat veered towards shore, where it rode the breakers onto a long stretch of sand. Sam and Joan and Lee hauled the boat into the beach grass.

"Fort Point," Sam said. "All ashore that's going ashore."

Lee and Joan emphatically said yes.

"Even with only half a plan?" Sam said.

"Totally," they both said.

"Totally, it is, dudes," Sam said.

"You're coming with us?" Lee asked.

"Wouldn't miss it for the world," he said.

"Excellent," Joan said.

Lee led the way up the beach dunes, slanting towards Fort Point. Maybe half a mile to go. This was where they had started.

Tramping along the dark cliffs of the seawall road, Lee heard a familiar voice from behind them.

"Sam, please! Sam, wait!"

Lee turned to look. The mysterious stranger, all dressed in black and closing fast.

"Hurry, hurry," Sam called. "We've got to make it to the fort."

Lee broke into a run, Joan on his heels. They were really moving now.

A tuft of beach strawberry found Lee's foot and caught it, and he tripped, headed face-first towards the swiftly tilting planet.

TWELVE

A Near Miss – Great to the
Fourth Power – The Miracle of Pizza –
That Darn Mysterious Stranger

The first thing Joan noticed? The fog. This was thick evening fog, and it was orange-blue, and it blew all around them. Next? It was cold. Then the ground beneath her feet—no longer sand and beach grass. Concrete, smooth and solid.

And the lights. The blue-white fluorescents and the red and yellow and green neon smudged beacons in the foggy evening. Orange sodium streetlights washed the sky. Evening? Hadn't it just been midnight?

The noise, too—the chatter and gab of a street scene, the whoosh of tires on pavement. Somewhere nearby, a siren; farther off, more sirens.

A MUNI bus squealed to a halt in front of them. Its doors hissed open. People jostled around her and streamed onto the bus.

Was she home?

They'd been moving towards Fort Point, and suddenly there was the stranger again, calling them, and they started running, Joan close behind Lee, and Lee tripped, and Joan reached for him, grabbed his sleeve, then she tripped, too, and closed her eyes against the fall. When she opened them—fog.

They were back in Chinatown, San Francisco, but much closer to *her* San Francisco, not Sam's. With any luck, they had overshot 2012 and landed somewhere around 2022, when all the stupid stuff that had crept into Joan's life would be long past. The world around her looked familiar, but how much difference could ten years make?

Lee and his big goofy grin stared up at the Chinatown buildings. He was saying, "Oooh, oooh."

Sam was plastered against the wall of a grocery store. Joan could see that he was trying to appear casual, relaxed. But the way his hands gripped the hem of his jacket and his stare fixed on the MUNI bus, she knew his calm was all an act.

The doors of the MUNI bus hissed closed, and it waddled up the street. The prongs that connected the bus to the overhead electric wires bounced roughly, and a bright sparking lit up the air. For a moment, the foggy world was a curtain of blue-green light.

Joan and Lee looked at each other. OKEY DOKE THEN.

Lee moved to Sam, put his hand on his sleeve.

"It's. O. Kay. Sam." Lee spoke loudly and slowly. "These. Are. Cars. This. Is. The. Fu. Ture."

Joan hit him a lick. "He's not deaf, you doofus," she said, "he's just unstuck."

Sam laughed now and slapped his knee. "Chill the pill, my young dudes," he said. "I've been to a future or two like this. I know about automobiles and aeroplanes and computing machines and such. I've seen some things. It simply takes a moment to adjust."

"You've been this far into the future?" Joan said.

"Maybe not this particular now. But close enough. You'd be surprised how much one future can be like another."

What *was* the date? Joan ran to a trash can and plucked a newspaper out of it. Scanned the top of the page. Gulped.

July 27, 2013. Only a year into her future. Not even close to where she hoped to find herself.

"It's two-thousand *thirteen*. July," she said out loud.

Lee snatched the paper from her. Then he looked

around Chinatown, as if there were answers written in the fog.

Lee was clearly disappointed. He looked up at Joan, and they shared the NO LOOK again, nothing communicated. She did not like this LOOK. Lee was hiding something from her; she was hiding something from him. Lee stomped to the trash can and stuffed the newspaper in it.

A big idea sliced through Joan's disappointment. It was such a big idea she'd forgotten to consider it in any of her time-travel plans. She had imagined that if she could get to 2022 or so, not only would she avoid the ugly parts of her future, but she could simply walk into that future and take up her new life. But she was still thirteen, not twenty-three, as she'd hoped. She hadn't counted on that.

If this was 2013, maybe there were two Joans in this San Francisco, the 2012 version *and* the 2013. Was one of those Joans fourteen years old now? What would happen if the two Joans met? The future might change, she supposed, or the past. The universe might collapse. *Star Trek* stuff.

"Sam," was all she could say.

The fog blew around them in great sheets; it was hard to see to the end of the block.

"Well, now, this is troubling," Sam said. He unglued himself from the grocery. "Whenever I land on a strange shore, I find it helpful to hunker down and take my bearings. I think I know just the place. Can you get us to Pacific and Stockton?"

They were at the corner of Grant and Jackson. Nothing was far from anything in Chinatown.

"That way," Joan said, pointing north. "Where are we going?"

"A friendly face," Sam said, "one you may even recognize."

Lee was staring off, thinking about something else but paying just enough attention that he managed to follow.

This Chinatown, *hers*, seemed so strange to Joan, having seen that other one, the shadow-man Chinatown.

As they walked along, Lee snapped out of his haze and became Sam's tour guide to the future. He pointed out all the future he could think of. That was an ATM. That was a cell phone. This was a cash register, this a stoplight.

It occurred to Joan that Sam might stand out in this crowd. Not because he wasn't Chinese. Neither was Lee. That made no difference in 2013 Chinatown. But what about his clothes, would they be a giveaway? Then Joan smiled. You'd have to dress a lot weirder than Sam to get noticed here. Sam looked like he might be a member of one of her favorite bands, Barbary Coast.

They turned left on Pacific, headed up its steep incline.

"There," Sam called. He pointed to a narrow shop across the street: Gim Chang's Herb and Ginger. A bell above the front door announced their entrance.

This was not the herb shop she used to visit with her father, but it was familiar. The high wooden drawers, the long counter, the glass jars. The shop seemed like— but could not possibly be—the one they'd been to earlier that night. Or 148 years ago—make that 149.

A man about as old as her father stepped out of the backroom. He wore an impeccable blue suit with a gold tie. He and Sam smiled at each other, then shook hands fiercely. Old friends.

Joan *did* recognize him. This man might be the Gim who had helped them earlier that night. But a much younger version.

Joan looked at Lee, saw in his eyes that he recognized Gim, too.

BRAIN FREEZE.

"Gim Chang, my dear friend."

"Sam. How unexpected," the man said. "As it always is."

"Gim. My good friends Joan and Lee."

The man shook hands with them.

"Welcome," Gim Chang said. "What brings you here this cold and foggy summer night?"

"We've come a bit unstuck, I'm afraid. Lee and Joan here came unstuck in my San Francisco. But they're from very close to here, 2012, just a bit off the mark."

"Hmm," Gim said vaguely. "A near miss."

"We were hoping," Sam said, "to stop in and get our bearings. Oh, and you'll appreciate this, they have recently met Great to the Fourth. We saw him earlier this evening."

Gim did nothing but smile. Then he locked the front door, turned the OPEN sign to CLOSED, and lowered the blinds.

"You *are* him," Lee said. "You saved our lives tonight."

This *was* the same herbalist who had saved them from the Kearny Street butchers only a few hours ago. It had to be.

"Nearly," Sam said. "Nearly. That Gim is the great-great-great-great"—Sam counted four fingers—"grandfather of this Gim. We call him Great to the Fourth."

"But, Sam," Joan said. "Why didn't—I mean, how—I mean . . ."

Just when she thought she had time travel figured out, she found there was still more to learn.

The green tea Gim served warmed Joan's body, but the rest of her remained fog frozen. This was not the *when* she had wanted, and it wasn't even home. Now what? Lee, too, seemed pretty frozen, staring into his blue-and-white cup.

But Gim and Sam had tons to say. Sam caught up Gim on his travels in the unstuck and Joan and Lee's adventures, too.

Sam pulled out his pipe, but this was the twenty-first century. Gim pointed to the back door.

"A disgusting habit, smoking," Gim said. "Don't you agree? No matter how many times I tell him, Sam still doesn't believe that in the future smoking is simply not allowed indoors. I love making him stand outside, his punishment for being an idiot."

Sam opened the back door, and for just a second, a keen vertigo perched on Joan's shoulder. She instantly saw the other Gim's alley from earlier that night. If Sam stepped through that door, he might disappear. But there was no alley here, just a tiny courtyard filled with garbage cans.

Sam leaned in the doorway, lit his pipe.

"I met Gim here first. During one of my trips, I stumbled into his shop. But that was twenty years ago for Gim, though we've shared other times together. I had been unstuck for only a week or two, when I met him, but he was younger then. It was my first time into a future so far ahead of my own I could not conceive of it. Apparently I was standing in front of the herb shop, looking as addlebrained as a school-board member. Now, Gim here, was by then a veteran of the big unstuck, and he recognized the look on my face. He kindly reeled me in and gave me shelter."

Gim smiled broadly, bowed his head.

"Sam here," Gim said, "is rather new to the unstuck. I started when I was twelve and am now nearly forty-five. Sam, you're what, twenty-eight? He's only been unstuck—by his own internal calendar—for a short time."

"Believe it's six weeks now," Sam said. "Hard to keep count."

"I did my best," Gim said, "to assure him that he would one day return to his own time. I did. We all eventually do. Soon after that, Sam met up with Great to the Fourth."

"But," Sam said, "I actually didn't meet Great to the Fourth in 1864. I met him during another unstuck, when I landed in 1857. When I saw him tonight, I hadn't seen him in years. Or weeks, depending on how you count it."

A silence crept into the room, circled a few times, then settled down. Joan was staring into her porcelain cup, at the flecks of tea leaves in the bottom.

Sam packed away his pipe and closed the back door. "What's gone with you two?" he said. "Here Gim and I are, entertaining you up one side of the barn and down the other, and you look like you're attending your own funerals."

"But—" Joan began, then clamped herself shut. She looked off into a corner. She'd almost blurted out her disappointment at being in this particular now. "But how do we get back? I mean, we're close, but this isn't horseshoes. Do we need to head for Fort Point?" AGAIN? "I just . . ."

"Well, now," Sam said, but that sentence never found its other half. He looked to Gim.

"Impossible to tell," Gim said with an apologetic smile. "You have to understand, Joan, none of us—not even Great to the Fourth—knows much about being unstuck. There's no time machine to dial up. No owner's manual to offer answers. There is only experience."

"That is so very helpful," Joan said, and not in a particularly polite fashion.

"Joan!" Sam said, scolding.

"I understand the frustration," Gim said. "Such a mystery is hard to accept. Sam'll tell you that. But my experience tells me all unstuckers get restuck. Sooner or later."

"Sooner or later?" Joan said.

"It's simple," Lee said out of his big silence. "We do what we just did. Go forward until something happens. Make something happen."

Lee was no longer staring into his teacup. He was pacing the backroom, touching stuff, his back to everyone. Joan couldn't tell if he was furious or on the edge of tears.

"Sitting here won't help," he said. "Sam showed us around his San Francisco, so it's only polite to show him around ours. Maybe we'll come unstuck again."

"Splendid," Sam said, "maybe tomorrow—"

"Now," Lee said. "We have to go now."

"But what if I run into myself?" Joan asked. "I mean, am I even out there, in 2013? Or are my parents still looking for me? Is my face on milk cartons and bus ads?"

"You are out there," Gim said. "Every self you've ever been, past and future, exists all at once. Why, fourteen-year-old Joan is probably having dinner with her family right now."

"But what if we go out there, and I see me?" Joan asked. "Won't I freak myself out?"

"Oh," Gim said, "that'd be just fine. You see, being you, that Joan would remember having run into you tonight."

She could almost see it. If they went outside, and Joan did run into herself, that would be the fourteen-year-old version of herself, who when she was thirteen and was busy being unstuck, ran into her older self. That future Joan might answer a lot of questions.

"Have you ever met yourself?" Joan asked Gim.

"Coming and going," he said.

"Sam?" Joan asked.

"Not as of yet," Sam said, and he knocked on wood.

"So, let's go," Lee said. "I'm dying to get back to the past."

Or the future, Joan thought.

Just in case they did come unstuck again, they decided to take their soldier's backpack with them, but before Lee could shoulder it, Joan dug into it for her Kixes. From the secret compartment in one heel, she pulled two slightly moist twenty dollar bills, the emergency fund her mother always put there. Now that they were *near* their own time, the money would come in handy.

"Just in case," Joan said, and she suddenly heard her mother's voice in hers.

Gim let them out the shop's front door and gave Sam a key. He wasn't coming with them.

"Not in the mood," Gim said, "for coming unstuck. I would only hold you back. I'm quite enjoying my now."

Joan said good-bye and pulled the slouch hat over her face.

"You won't be needing that," Gim said. "This is your San Francisco. Ours."

He waved them off into the fog-soaked night.

As they headed down the hill towards Stockton, into Chinatown's shopping crush, Lee kept running ahead in little bursts, with floppy arms and feet, apparently trying to come unstuck again. He looked like a determined ostrich.

Sam and Joan hung back, content to watch Lee being silly.

"So," Joan said to Sam. "I see Gim's point. He's not up for coming unstuck again. But why did you come with us, Sam? In the first place? Don't you want to stay stuck in your own time?"

"Adventure," was all Sam said.

"C'mon, Sam," Joan said. "It's more than that. I can tell."

"My civic duty?" he said. "Make sure you whipper-snappers get home in one piece. Ease my conscience."

A few paces ahead of them, Lee, flapping and flopping, trying to unstick himself, fell. Down hard on both knees. Man, that had to hurt.

"We appreciate your concern," Joan said to Sam, "we really do. But there's something else. You 'cast off,' too, without knowing when or how you'd ever get back to where you're supposed to be."

Joan gave Sam her very best FESS UP, and Joan's FESS UP was a mighty powerful LOOK.

They were on Stockton now. The grocers and restaurant and shops all crawling. The San Francisco of 1864 had seemed crazy busy to Joan, but nothing compared to this. The world just kept getting busier.

"Because I love it," Sam said. "Oh, I love my own time, too, that one true life of mine, the one I live day to day." He looked over at Joan, slyly.

"But I love the Great Unstuck, too. I love to see as much as I can. How people live. How things change; how they don't. I want to know everything, see everywhere. Every *when*."

Given the crowds on Stockton, it was impossible for Lee to flap and fly now, so he turned his attention to running into things—corners, lampposts, MUNI shelters.

"At first," Sam went on, "I thought it was my duty as a writer, to see and know everything. If I am to become Mark Twain, I figure it best to know as much as possible about the world and the people who live in it. But the more I see, the more I realize it's not just a writer's job. It's a person's job. It behooves us all to be interested in other people."

Sam was itching for his pipe now, Joan saw. Lee, well, Lee had just tried to trip himself on a parking meter.

"Like now," Sam said. "This is my favorite kind of unstuck. With friends, on a straight quarter of river. Cruising along, watching. Taking in this lovely evening in this wondrous city, simply for the here-ness of it."

Although she had been craving a leap into the 2022 future, Joan found she could shut her brain to that urgency. For the moment, at least, it was good to be here. If only to watch Lee being a doofuzoid.

Part of the calm Joan now felt was from Chinatown itself. This Chinatown, a place she once thought she knew—and thought a little boring—was suddenly fresh in her eyes. What she'd seen of San Francisco in 1864 opened her eyes to what it was in 2013.

So, she told Sam all about the place. This San Francisco was a city that was half Chinese, or at least, Chinese-American. The Chinese community practically *owned* San Francisco. The Chinese were no longer afraid to show their faces, no longer shadow people, no longer deprived of their families. And here, in the heart of Chinatown, even the language prevailed. All the signs, even the street signs, were written in Chinese characters. Joan watched the shoppers around her, almost all, to one degree or another, of Chinese descent. The fear had been banished.

She pointed out to Sam a young couple and their stroller-strapped baby. The mother was Chinese, the father some form of white. The baby was beautiful. Everyone looked happy.

"I could really use a slice," Lee said. "I needs me a slice."

PIIIZZZAAA.

At Columbus, they turned south into North Beach. There was the Transamerica Pyramid, looming in front of them. From its apex, a red signal light pulsed slowly. It reminded Joan of the lighthouse at Fort Point. Were such lights meant to warn sailors away, or draw them near?

Lee tried his best to describe to Sam the precise nature of pizza.

"A pie, you say?" Sam wasn't getting the picture.

At the North Beach Pizza takeout window on Grant, Joan ordered three combo-meat-veggie slices and three

Cokes, and they stationed themselves at the narrow bar that clung to the outside of the building.

Sam went gaga over the pizza. He ate and proclaimed all at once.

"Now this," he said, lifting the slice into the air. "This is a miracle. Never has there been such a food. And you can eat it with one hand. With your fingers. Oh. Ah. If pizza is in the future, then the future may be worth having after all."

Joan had to agree with Sam. The pizza was wicked good. Lee was too busy eating to offer an opinion.

Sam took a sip of his Coke and spit it out, ska-bloosh, right on the sidewalk.

"That is a vile concoction," Sam said. "And you two think smoking is disgusting?" Sam shuddered. "One problem with the future is that the good and the bad arrive together. Unavoidable. Like this miraculous pizza and this so-called beverage. You can see this paradox in rivers, where a clear blue tributary arrives at a confluence with a muddy, mucky channel. The two colors swirl together, but remain separated. Still the same river."

"Sam," a voice called from down the street.

Sam froze.

Joan knew the voice. It had called to them in front of the opera house, and on the seawall road by Fort Point. Joan looked. There was the mysterious stranger she and Lee had both seen. He was an unstucker, too. This could not be a good thing.

Sam was looking directly at the stranger. In addition to being frozen, he was now white. Yep, like a ghost.

"Sam," the man called again, trying to squirm through the crowd.

"Butchers," Sam whispered. And they were off to the races, running, towards Gim's.

Joan tried to go as fast as she could and still keep her eyes on the ground. To come unstuck or not, that was a tricky question.

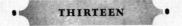

THIRTEEN

Cars vs. Guns – Now What? – Two Travelers at Odds – Instruments of Extreme Power – Lessons in Relativity

If he could somehow transport the theory and practice of pizza-making back to Sam's San Francisco, then, Lee thought, he would live there happily. Having compared 1864 to 2013, he didn't find real advantages to 2013. The only thing 1864 lacked was pizza. And maybe burritos—burritos would be good, too. And to be honest, the "toilet" facilities of 1864 did leave a lot to be desired. But on the whole, Lee preferred the past.

At first, he had felt some relief at being back in a future so close to his own. Then the disappointment set in. Lee had been wishing really hard to end up in 2007 or so, with time to change his parents' minds about the future, bring them together again. Somehow. But no matter how much he tripped and flew and collided on that walk, wishing to come unstuck, he and Joan and Sam remained in 2013.

Though this San Francisco was quite similar to his own, Lee couldn't help but see his world in a brand-new way. The first thing that struck him about 2013 was a distinct lack of handguns, rifles, and cannons, not to mention cleavers and other weapons. Everyone in 1864, including the Misses Greta and Penelope, carried some form of firepower. Didn't that make Sam's world a more dangerous place?

As they made their way through Chinatown and North Beach, however, Lee was stunned, then frightened by the many cars and trucks and buses and motorcycles, and how dangerously fast and huge and metallic they were. No one in 1864 fired their guns over and over down the street, but cars flew everywhere and continually in 2013.

This future San Francisco was more crowded, too, and as Sam had said of other futures he'd visited, louder and brighter. It was also sharper and concrete-ier, and generally more fraught with peril, Lee considered.

Then the mysterious stranger showed up, and the whole debate over which San Francisco was more dangerous seemed to be settled in Lee's mind. Lee wasn't quite sure he bought Sam's theory that this was one of the butchers. Hadn't he and Joan both seen the mysterious stranger *before* they'd ever heard about the butchers? Besides, they'd lost the stranger in the Chinatown crowds.

But sitting in the herb shop's backroom again, with more tea, along with some pretty tasty almond cookies, none of Lee's thoughts on the safety versus the danger of various times seemed to matter at all. They had not come unstuck again; they were trapped. How was he supposed to change his future when he was stuck in it?

Joan, for her part, was grilling Sam about the stranger—she was quite upset. Under other circumstances, Lee probably would have joined in, but whether or not this was an unstuck butcher seemed less urgent a matter to Lee than being marooned in a time he had no desire to be in.

Lee kept opening his mouth to speak, to say, "Hey, can we talk about the future or the past or whatever anything is now," but Joan was locked and loaded, and there was very little hope of Lee getting a word in edgewise. Seated across the table from Lee, Gim smiled a quiet, sympathetic smile, one that said to Lee, "I've got a bossy older sister. I know how you feel."

Lee returned a quiet, resigned WORD. Gim nodded. WORD.

"Why didn't you tell us," Joan was saying, "that the butchers could come unstuck?"

"I cannot tell you," Sam said, clearly irritated with Joan, "what I did not yet know. And he ruined my pizza."

"But a butcher, coming unstuck? How is that possible?" Joan was pressing down on the table as if it were made of helium and might float away.

Sam's hands fluttered around his head. "It's never been proved," he said, "that a bad man couldn't come unstuck. Nor a bad woman. Coming unstuck don't necessarily make you a good person. Just different." Sam eased off, his hands at rest in the pockets of his waistcoat, and he leaned back in his chair. "Why, I recall," he went on, "once in Nevada City, I was talking to a man who swore his bird, this irascible blue jay, could—"

"Sam Clemens," Joan said, and she slapped the table. "Enough of your tall tales. Every time you start a tall tale, you lean back and drawl, and next thing you know, the truth's about five miles down the road."

She leaned over the table. Glaring. Lee was really quite fed up and wanted to tell Joan to get over it, move on, forget the stranger. But he knew better than to take her on right now.

Sam had leaned forward, too, his hands flat on the table, and he glared right back at Joan, as good as she gave. Their noses were less than a foot apart. While there was no yelling or talking, a long, complex, and intense conversation was being conducted. All with LOOKS. Joan accused; Sam defended. Joan rationalized; Sam re-accused.

Lee looked over at Gim with the old HOLY MACKEREL, but Gim merely watched this battle, his arms crossed.

Sam relented. He pushed back from the table, his hands surrendering. Joan, gloating a bit—she was a *terrible* winner—tossed Sam a LOOK that was much too easy to read. TAKE THAT.

"What?" Sam said. "What do you want, you iron-jawed, brass-mouthed, copper-bellied . . ."

He'd run out. Defeated.

"I think you're keeping something from us," Joan said, "and I don't like it. That stranger just now. I don't think that's any kind of butcher at all. Lee and I saw him before, before the word butcher meant anything to us. I saw that look on your face back there, and I think you know exactly who it is. You need to tell us right now."

All the silence in Gim's herb shop gathered into a dense cloud that hung over the backroom table.

"Lee," Joan said. YOU WITH ME?

The only thing Lee had on offer was the NO LOOK,

and this was certainly the darkest, most complicated NO LOOK of them all. In this NO LOOK was, "I don't care about the stranger, I don't care what you need to know right now, I don't really care about getting back 'home,' I don't care if you find out the secret I've been keeping from you, and I don't care anymore whatever secret it is you are hiding from me. All I care about is changing my future."

The NO LOOK Joan returned to Lee was as blank and unknowable as the one he gave her.

"That's it," Gim said, snapping his fingers, suddenly spry. "Secrets. You're all keeping secrets from one another. You and you, and you, too, Sam. That's why you near missed, I'd wager. Now, the Misses Greta and Penelope, who have always traveled together—"

"You know the misses?" Lee said.

"Everyone knows them," Gim said. "The misses have learned that such secrets make it hard to find the right time. What's that saying of yours, Sam, too many oars, not enough rudders?"

It all crashed down on Lee. Gim was right. Lee'd kept his plan a secret. If he'd let Joan and Sam in on it, maybe they wouldn't have ended up here. Maybe Lee's plan—to go to his past and change his future—was keeping them stuck where none of them wanted to be.

"Fine," Lee said. He never was good at keeping secrets; this one might be his world record. "I *have* been keeping a secret. I do not want to go back to 2012. This whole time I've been wanting to go back to the past. Like to when I was eight, when my family was really happy. I figured I could change something there, and then my parents would stay together, and life wouldn't look so stupid. I thought I might even change Joan's parents' minds about high schools. I want to change the past."

Lee took a big gulp, then looked at Joan, ready for her assault. She didn't seem angry, though, only embarrassed.

"Well, uh," Joan said, turning her hands palm up on the table. "I, uh, kind of have a secret, too. I didn't really want to go back to 2012, either. I thought we'd just skip all that and scoot on ahead. Like 2022 or so, all grown-up, all that divorce and school blech behind us. Right?"

Sam tapped a beat on the table—ba-dum. He looked at Gim and laughed. Gim's smile retreated a bit.

"That explains it," Sam said. "Too many oars, not enough rudders. You both want it all. But you can't have one without the other. You can't change the past. You can't skip into the future. There's only one river, and by gum, one way or another, you've got to travel it. I told you before—the misses told you, Gim's telling you—being unstuck, that just gives us a bigger picture of the river. But you've still got to float it, every bend and hazard."

Sam seemed quite pleased. Gim did not.

"And you, Sam?" Gim said. "Your secret?"

"Everything I know about secrets," Sam said, pushing back from the table, "I learned from a riverboat gambler name of Ray Jim John, a man we called the Heckler. One August, just outside of—"

"Sam!" This was Lee and Joan and Gim as one, as if rehearsed.

Sam hung his head. "Truth is," he said, "that stranger tonight was no butcher. A known fact. That man, whoever he is, has been following me for some time. Round about my second or third unstuck, he appeared. I do not know him, and I do not trust him. He calls my name, and I get the shivers—what we call the fantods. Like when a ghost walks over your grave. Then he's gone."

A shudder, cold and prickly, ran down the entire length of Lee's body. All the way to his toes. Lee sensed the same shudder run through Joan. "But now what?" Lee shook off his shudder.

"We try again," Sam said, "to come unstuck. Every story I know worth the lard to fry it up—"

"Sam!" Joan, of course.

"Bear with me," he said. "My down-home has its purposes. As I was saying, every good story is nothing more than a series of mistakes made by the main characters, until they finally find the right way."

That made a whole bunch of sense to Lee.

Joan started to speak, then restarted.

"I got nothin'," she said. A first for Joan. "Not a single idea of how to go forward from here."

"If I may," Gim said. "I have an idea and, better yet, instruments of extreme power to aid you in your quest."

Instruments of extreme power? Now, they were talking. Magic wands, enchanted swords, luminous crystals. That's what was needed. Lee could deal with this—about time.

Gim went to the front of the store, and when he returned, he was hiding something in his hand.

"These will transport you to your desired destination in no time at all."

He revealed three glittering objects.

"I give you," Gim said, "the MUNI Fast Pass." With a flourish, he fanned the bus passes like cards in a magic trick.

Lee and Joan shared a funny but confused LOOK. JEEPERS.

Gim's plan was simple. They would all spend the night at the herb shop and, in the morning, go out again but towards Lee's house, or Joan's. If they wanted to get back home, then home seemed as good a direction as any. Better, actually.

But Sam and Gim insisted, Joan and Lee had to be in accord. They both had to want to get back to 2012, want to get restuck in time.

"Dudes?" Sam wanted to know.

"I swear to it," Joan said.

"I swear, too," Lee said. He was no longer keeping a secret. He was flat out lying.

A bove Gim's shop was a guest apartment he kept for visiting family and the odd unstucker. Joan and Lee would share the bedroom—twin beds—while Sam slept in the living room on a fold-out couch. Gim insisted on sleeping on a cot in the shop's backroom, in case any strangers came calling.

Joan coerced Lee to take a shower, and he had to admit it was great to be clean again. When he was done, Joan hopped in and took a shower Lee estimated long enough to use up every last drop of hot water in San Francisco.

Lee lay in his narrow bed and prepared himself for a sleepless night. He imagined that between devising a plan to change his past and his guilt over his decision to leave Joan on her own, he'd be awake forever. But the instant Joan crawled into her bed and turned off the light, Lee felt himself crashing down through the layers of wakefulness. He didn't even have time to worry if he'd be in the same *when* when he woke up. He slept. He had had too much to think.

It was foggy, of course, when he woke, but from the soft pearly light that came through the curtains, Lee could gauge the time. Latish, about ten. Joan stirred but did not rouse. He'd slept in his clothes again, and so it was easy to pocket the MUNI Fast Pass, sneak down the stairs, and let himself out the front door. Gim had left his keys on the backroom table, and both he and Sam were snoring up such storms, a rhino could have charged through without waking them. He was outside in a flash.

He had to wait a few minutes for the 30 Stockton, but there it was and not too crowded. As the bus pulled away, heading into the Stockton Tunnel, Lee walked towards the backseats, his preferred MUNI position.

And there was Joan, out the back window, running towards the bus stop. She was waving and waving, calling something. Frantic.

There was so much motion going on, Lee didn't really know for a moment where he stood. The bus was moving forwards, but Lee was walking to the back of it, and there was Joan, running towards him. For a few seconds, Lee and Joan stayed still, the only still points in the universe, everything else moving around them. They stared across that space at each other.

But the bus picked up speed, Lee reached the back-seat, and Joan slowed to a halt. It was unstoppable now. They were moving away from each other.

Lee wasn't at all sure he would ever see her again. What was that LOOK? GOOD-BYE.

FOURTEEN

Alone in the Future – The Magic Forest – A Brand-New Car – A Thief in the House

L ee Bartholomew Jones was a little rat. And if Joan ever caught him, he'd be a dead little rat.

How dare he! Leave her alone like this, stuck in a future neither one of them wanted. He *had* been keeping a secret from her, she just knew it, and a *huge* secret at that. Sure, she'd been keeping one from him, too. The little rat.

Sam had found Joan stomping and snorting at the bus stop just as Lee's bus was disappearing into the darkness of the Stockton Tunnel. Sam had figured out Lee's evasive maneuver and didn't need to be convinced that the little rat was probably headed for his house.

They ran back to Gim's, borrowed a little extra cash, and hailed a passing cab.

The cab ride was probably a huge freak-out for Sam, the whole "automobile" thing, but Joan didn't have time to worry about him. She was too busy devising horrible ways to punish Lee. And she was too busy, too, trying to argue with time. It would take at least twenty minutes to get to Lee's, but the traffic was bad this morning. Joan stared out the taxi's window and fumed as the taxi crept through the car-packed streets. One thing was certain about traffic: You could not make it go faster.

But along with her frustration, what she saw from the taxi was that the past, present, and future all lived together in this one San Francisco. It showed itself in the houses they passed. Often in the same block, occasionally right next to one another, were houses built well over a hundred years ago, houses built since the earthquake of 1906, and all the years in between, along with houses out of weird science-fiction futures. Gingerbread Victorians, stucco boxes, twisted space stations. All times here in one.

However, interesting as this observation was to Joan, it didn't keep her from growing more furious with Lee. Little rat? Big rat.

But her furiosity disappeared when they got to Lee's neighborhood, Eighth Avenue and Irving. There was the Crepevine, Amazing Fantasy Comics, Crossroad Clothing, Pasquale's Pizza, and, oh, her favorite, Tutti Frutti Toys for All Ages. And halfway down Eighth, Lee's house. How many times had Joan walked up to this house? Lee's tall and skinny house. Pale sandy yellow, dark red trim, green roof. No front yard. Sandwiched between two identical houses, no space between them. Joan had forgotten that the roof was green. Had forgotten how happy a house could make her.

But no Lee in sight. Suddenly she was neither angry nor fascinated nor relieved. She was frantic.

When she and Sam got to Lee's driveway, they found the door to the side corridor open. Lee must have gone down here, where the trash cans were kept, to see if he could get in the back way—he still didn't have his own key.

Suddenly, there was Lee, right in front of her. He was running straight at her, and he was being chased by some teenage boy.

"Joan, run," Lee said.

Just as he said it, he was gone. Not quite in an instant, a snap. But gone nonetheless.

It was as if Lee were tethered to a leash. He pulled up short and kind of disappeared. It wasn't like the bad TV version of disappearing, where the character was edited out—there, not there. Or like a *Star Trek* transporter, all glittery and slow. A little of both, to tell the truth. Lee faded like smoke but quickly. Exactly as the mysterious stranger had faded. Lee was there one minute, and then Joan was sort of looking through him, and then he was not there.

"No!" yelled the boy who'd been chasing Lee.

Joan backed up into Sam, and Sam was backing away, too, pulling her by her jacket collar out of the narrow corridor. In another moment, she knew, they'd be turned around and running away from this boy.

But before that could happen, the boy disappeared just as Lee had, a figure of quickly faded smoke. Only space where he'd recently been.

Joan could only stare.

Lee had come unstuck again. And so had the boy who was chasing him. That part was simple.

Other parts were not. *When* had Lee gone to? And did the boy go there, too?

Sam still had ahold of her jacket collar, and he was pulling them up the driveway, and now they were headed down the foggy street, towards the tall tree line of Golden Gate Park only half a block away.

Joan walked faster and faster, barely stopping at the crosswalk on Lincoln. Sam put out a hand to slow her, but she was running now, across Lincoln, then up into the Magic Forest. She was on the edge of tears or screaming or very possibly both.

She came to a breathless halt in a small meadow between two rows of trees, the Magic Forest. Lee and Joan used to come here to sit on the bench of a fallen eucalyptus and hang out. They never shared this place with anyone else; they pinkie swore on that.

Now there were tears on her face, her fists were clenched, and she was indeed about ready to scream.

She spun on Sam. If she was going to scream, she might as well have someone to scream at.

"What the—"

Sam stopped her. He yelled over her scream, "I don't know, Joan! I don't know."

Joan froze.

She wiped her tears on her sleeve. Gulped down air. It was quiet here in the Magic Forest.

"I wish I knew, Joan," Sam said. Softly. "I wish I knew where he was. I wish I knew when we'd see him again. I wish I knew what to do next. But I don't." Sam looked spooked. And you know what? That did not help.

"What do we do?" She was whispering now.

"We could wait," Sam said. "Wait by his house, see if he returns. Or go back to Gim's."

Joan—much, much later in her life—would always be amazed by the memory of standing here with Sam—Mark Twain—in the Magic Forest. She would always look back with wonder at how quickly she had moved from bewilderment to shock to fear to anger, and then to courage and the calm that came with courage.

"No," she said. "Let's go to my house. At least I know *where* I'm going."

They could cut through the park, then catch the 33 at Arguello, which would take them right near her house.

It would be good to be home again, no matter the year. The house, at least, should still be there, something solid.

At the next crosswalk, the blue Corolla apparently didn't see the stop sign and Joan, obviously, did not see the Corolla. But Sam saw the car in the nick of time, and he yanked Joan back from the street.

She fell on her butt. Ow, that would leave a mark.

She'd landed in a puddle and was really hoping it was only water. You never knew in the park. It was okay—it was raining, so it must be rainwater.

But it wasn't raining.

Oh, it was raining. And she was in her backyard at home, and there was no sign of Sam.

She bolted up from the ground.

Raining? Check. Backyard? Check. All alone? Double check. Okay? Not really.

If it was raining, she knew she was no longer in the same *when*. She'd just been in July 2013. It never rained in San Francisco in July. Tons of fog but no rain. And this rain, she recognized, was a good spring drenching. A steady rain, diligent. A little cold. The sky was a gray-black plate suspended over the city. The grass of the backyard was sharp green, and the trees of the Presidio on the other side of the stone fence, they were lush green, blooming. If she had to guess, she'd say this was March.

The light of the day was different, too. It had just been morning, but it seemed late afternoon now.

A late afternoon in March. Good guess. But which year?

She looked up at her house. There was her bedroom window. Nothing seemed to have changed much. Those were the same curtains, at least. Turquoise blue. They'd been put up a few months before the field trip.

If only there were some way to see into her room. Uh . . .

Meaning she could be seen. She was standing in the middle of the backyard. Anyone could see her. She could almost hear her older—or possibly younger—self calling out to her family, "Hey, you guys, there's some-one in the backyard, and she looks really familiar."

Joan zipped over to the side yard, where the garbage cans were kept. Right next to the door that led into the garage was a fake rock—it wouldn't fool anyone it was so fake—and Joan lifted it. In the hollow of the fake rock was the "secret" key. Definitely the right house.

She figured it was safe enough to go into the garage, at least get out of the rain. But as she was slipping the key into the lock, the garage door thrummed to life and began to rise.

Through the side door's window, she saw three cars. Her mom's BMW was still there and her sister Fiona's Honda. But her dad's black Mercedes had been replaced by a snazzy, lime green Prius. Didn't seem like her dad's kind of car at all.

Someone was coming from the kitchen into the ga-rage. Joan ducked away from the window but slowly al-lowed herself back up. Peeking in on her own life. Weird.

The girl was talking on the phone, jangling her keys. She stood by the Prius and stroked the roof of it with admiration.

"Ma, I know," this girl was saying into the cell. "I know. I promise. Yes, I turned off the stove. Yes, and the lights. I promise. Look, Ma, I gotta go. Bye."

The girl clicked her cell shut. Sighed like nobody's business. Then smiled at the car and got in.

Joan had not known until that moment that someone could look exactly like her and still seem a total stranger. How could Joan be both of these people at once?

The Prius pulled out. The garage door closed.

Oh, cool, Joan thought, I love that car. *My car.*

Oh, my God, Joan thought, I'm at least sixteen. Maybe not as far into future as she had hoped, but at least she had a car.

Lee was always telling Joan that she lived in a "ginormous" house. And she was always telling him that he was full of it. Her house, she told him, was just a regular house. Yes, there were more bedrooms in her house than in Lee's, but she had all those brothers and sisters. It evened out: Lee had more privacy.

The truth was that Joan preferred hanging out at Lee's house. Both his parents worked, and so in the afternoons, she and Lee often went to his place to "do homework." If by homework you meant watching *Planet Crankypants* on Cartoonia TV, or playing Omnicrush online, where Lee and Joan constructed entire civilizations only to destroy them with giant reptiles, nuclear armaments, and various ecological disasters. And, of course, there was much eating of snacks from Lee's over-stuffed pantry.

At Joan's house, day and night, life was a perpetual emergency. Someone was always having a crisis and being very loud about it—one of her brothers or one of her sisters or one of each or both of one or everybody—screaming and slamming doors. Then her dad would come home from work and the commotion started all over again. Even within the privacy of her bedroom, it was impossible to get away from her family's drama. When the arguments were over and the house returned to quiet, Joan could still feel the agitation, as if the ghosts of her family's arguments roamed the halls and banged on the doors.

At Lee's house, they sat on the sofa and watched TV and ate things that were bad for them and talked all afternoon. It was always best, Joan thought, when it was foggy outside. Lee's house was cozy to begin with, and the fog only made it cozier.

This was what she was thinking, standing in her family's kitchen. That she'd really rather be at Lee's house with him after an ordinary day at school. But she was here—let's see, at least 2015—in a strangely quiet house.

She turned into the living room, and it was like walking into a meadow: it was that big. There was a fireplace along one wall, big enough to roast a goat in. Another wall of the living room was all windows with a view of the Presidio. In the corner was a jade statue the size of a small dog, which happened to be a statue of a small dog. Around the statue's pedestal flowed acres of blond-wood floor. Lee was right; her house was ginormous.

Standing there in the nearly empty living room, Joan felt like weeping. She wasn't sure why, she just did. It all welled up inside her. It was almost too much to see her life from the outside like this. Where was Lee when she needed him?

Joan shook off the knot of tears and headed for her bedroom, up the long carpeted stairway, down the long hushed hall. The doorknob in her hand was electric.

Could she? She did.

Her room was surprisingly similar to when she'd left it—at least three years ago. The furniture was all the same, though her desk was over by the window, and the bed was lengthwise against the wall. That was a good idea, kind of like a couch with all those pillows.

The color scheme was the same—pale greens and aqua blues—but the bedspread was different, blue-and-green polka-dots on white. Very nice. But she'd added some orange accents that really gave a kick to the place—a couple of pillows and a throw rug. And there was one of those paper star lamps in swirly oranges and browns hanging from the ceiling. When she turned on the light, the room was cast in a plush glow. About time. She'd been planning to get one of those lamps for years.

Above her bed hung large hammocks of her stuffed animals, their little snouts and heads poking out. She was really glad to see them.

Her bulletin board. Same board, different souvenirs. This ought to be good.

The bulletin board was a jumble of ticket stubs, plastic beads, a couple of different to-do lists, pictures of bands cut out of music magazines, some weird anime characters, snapshots. The usual.

The first thing that drew her eye was a strip of four images from a photo booth. The pictures showed Joan goofing off and making silly faces with a girl she did not recognize. The girl had dyed, black hair with severe bangs, and she looked a little gothy, her wrists covered with silver bracelets. They were obviously close friends and still must be. Above the photo strip was a cheap-looking bracelet whose letter beads spelled out "Camille." Joan could not help but wonder when and where she would meet Camille.

Peeking out from under a note in her own writing that said, "What It Means Is What It Says!" Joan spotted another photo, the bottom half of a red formal dress.

She pushed the note out of the way, and there she was in a strapless gown, a white-rose corsage on her wrist. Next to her in a black tuxedo stood Lee. The computer-imposed caption read Spring Fling 2014. A formal. How cool.

But. Did that mean that she and Lee, were they . . . it's not that . . . she was just kind of . . . Lee, she had to admit, was looking pretty good in 2014. He had a sharp haircut.

She stared at the photo. She and Lee didn't seem particularly lovey-dovey. Hmmm. Really hard to read. It was weird, no matter how she sliced it.

Then she saw the envelope. It was tacked to the bottom of the bulletin board. A regular white envelope and written on it in her own handwriting: "For Joan @ 13 from Joan @ 16. Yes, you! Open me!"

Her hand shook when she took the envelope from the bulletin board.

No time like the present, she thought. This made her laugh a little. Apparently there were many times like the present.

She opened the letter.

Dear Joan,
I mean me. I mean us. You get it. This letter will be short. Don't stay too long. Ma will be home in a

little bit. And besides, I don't want to give away everything. The future should have some surprises.

I—you—always remember coming unstuck here on this day. It's March 3, 2015. We're sixteen years old. It's weird being here, isn't it? It's weird writing this letter, too. But when I woke up this morning and realized what day it was, I thought I'd write. There are a few things I want you to know, which I hope will make the next months easier for you.

Mom and Dad did get divorced. But it's a lot better now. Oh, the first year really sucks. There's a lot of screaming. But then it gets better. I've never seen Ma so happy, and I actually like hanging out with Dad. Every Friday night we have dinner together. Swanky. He's funnier than you think. So, take a deep breath and hang in there.

We do go to Starr King—couldn't get out of that. But it's okay, too. I like the kids a lot, and you're really gonna like Camille. You'll meet her freshman year, so not too long. Warning: She's a little annoying in the beginning but that changes.

And Lee likes her, too. I think he has kind of a crush on her but nothing serious. And that's what I really want to tell you. Lee and us, we're still best friends. Always have been. We cut school sometimes, still have lunch a lot at the Chinese place across from City. And he's a good date for dances. No. We're just friends.

In fact, that's where I was going when you got here—over to Lee's. We're gonna play Omnicrush all day.

That's all I'm gonna say right now. I want you to live your future first. But I felt I could tell you a few things. And don't even think of looking for your diary—we still keep one. It's in my purse.

Hey, here's an experiment. Keep this letter. Let's see what happens to it in three years. Will we have to write it all over again? This time thing—it's so weird.

Now, get out of here.

Your pal, You.

P.S. Don't you just love the car? It goes with the bedspread.

Joan thought she'd have to stare at this letter for a long time in order to take it all in. But the garage door shook the house with its low growl. Ma?

Joan folded the letter into her back pocket, turned off the lights, and padded down the stairs.

She knew where to go—this was her house after all. She cut behind the kitchen just as the door from the garage creaked open. Her mom was bringing groceries in from the car. Joan was dying to take one glance at her, one look at her future mom. But she couldn't risk it. Not that she could get into trouble. Joan hadn't really done anything wrong. The only laws she'd broken were the laws of physics, and they couldn't put you in jail for that, could they? No, it was just too weird, and she didn't want to freak Ma out. Joan could wait.

She slipped into the front hall, snuck out the front door, but pulling it shut, it got away from her and slammed hard. Joan just made it past the front gate of the house when she heard her mother calling out, "Who's there?"

Joan turned to look back at the house while running away from it, when—

This whole unstuck thing was starting to get annoying. Couldn't they make an announcement? "Time travel will commence in two minutes. All passengers will please . . ."

She had fallen to her knees on a sidewalk—really painful—and a woman was helping her up with a storm of "Are you okays?"

It was foggy again. Noon? She was in the Marina, Chestnut Street. Joan hoped, hoped, hoped this was 2013, the year when she'd last seen Lee and Sam. Maybe they were already back at Gim's. It was what she most wanted in the world right now, to see them both. Especially Lee.

Books Inc. was right down the block, so she dashed in and checked *The Chronicle*: July 28, 2013. All right! Familiar territory. She'd head back to the herb shop. This was really good news.

Before she left the store, she wanted to check one thing. In fiction, under T, she found *Huckleberry Finn*, *Tom Sawyer*, *Roughing It*, *Life on the Mississippi*, *A Connecticut Yankee in King Arthur's Court*. All by Mark Twain who had, the backs of the books said, been born Samuel Clemens. She knew the books had been written, she just needed to double-check.

On her way past the front counter, she spied a book that made her stop. It was the fifth book in the Heartless series by Jody Wellton, *As If It Were So*. The book would come out 2013, which was now. Awesome. If she ever got back to 2012, she'd be the first on her block to own it. Way first.

She still had some cash left from the taxi.

The young woman behind the counter said, "It just came in today. You're the first. I can't wait, either. I love Heartless." The woman's Books Inc. name tag read "Full Frontal Nerdity."

The clerk put a bookmark in *As If It Were So*, but

Joan saw something printed on the bookmark that made her pull it out. "Books, Inc. Since 1853, the West's Oldest Independent Bookseller." Really? Could it be? Joan took two more bookmarks—one for Sam and one for Lee—and skipped out of the store. She loved souvenirs.

FIFTEEN

Suddenlied! – His Best Guess – *Starcruiser Omega* – Talking to Yourself – Swing Set to the Stars

It wasn't that Lee didn't believe Sam when he told him that the past couldn't be changed. He simply didn't *want* to believe him. Lee was being stubborn, he knew, Joan-caliber stubborn, but what were you gonna do? Take your best shot. He didn't know if his plan would work—he barely knew anything for certain any longer, but he did know he had to try.

There was a moment—a very tough moment—when Joan was running after the bus, and Lee thought he might have to jump off and rejoin her. He was terrified he might never see her again. But he held his ground.

He was, he told himself, doing this as much for Joan's future as for his own. Once he figured out—*if* he figured out—how to change his own past, thereby changing his future, he could do the same for Joan's past and future. Everyone would be happy again. Stubborn? Yes. Crazy? Heck, yeah! Too late? Certainly. He had cast off.

So he swallowed that big lump of good-bye and stayed on the bus, and by the time he got to Market and transferred to the N Judah streetcar, his spirits had lifted. He was going where he wanted.

All during the streetcar ride, he sang to himself, a song he used to sing with his parents. "Let's do the time warp again!" It was from a really funny movie, *The Rocky Horror Picture Show*, but that's not where he knew it from. It was also the opening theme to a radio program, *10 @ 10*, where the deejay, Dave Morey, played "ten great songs from one great year." Lee and his parents listened to the show all the time, on KFOG, their favorite station. It was old people music, but Lee liked this music, especially the Beatles. His parents always ended up talking about whatever had happened to them during the year they were listening to—1974 or 1983 or 1998, whichever. They would all sit together in the living room on Saturday mornings and listen to the show and read the paper and just hang out and talk. But it had been a long time since they had listened to the show like that, as a family, all together.

Lee was psyched to see his house from the corner of Eighth and Irving, but as he approached it, he grew uneasy. He should be thrilled to be here but was more confused than thrilled. Was his fourteen-year-old self home? It was summer after all. Were his parents home? Or just his mom, or just his dad? Eek! Did he even live here anymore? He pushed aside his confusion. He had to pretend everything was going to be hunky-dory.

Lee went down the short slanted drive to the utility corridor, where the garbage cans were kept. There was a spare key hidden in the backyard. Lee moved forward into the dark hallway.

When he was almost to the end of the corridor, the back door opened, and a silhouette of some big kid suddenly appeared. Lee froze.

"Hey," this kid said. "I've been waiting for you."

Lee turned and darted towards the street. He could no longer pretend he was dealing.

Then he saw Joan at the far end of the corridor, Sam behind her. Lee was moving towards them when his jacket caught on an old nail and—yoink!—yanked him off his feet.

Suddenly, it was night. A clear sky, no moon. A few shreds of cloud.

Lee was in his backyard—suddenly. But now it was night, and he was, he thought, alone. Suddenly.

Everything was all suddenly these days.

Of course, the good thing about repeated suddenlies was that you did get used to them after a while. The nail caught his jacket, lifted him off the ground half a second, and Lee just had the time to think, Oh, here we go again. So, when—suddenly!—he was in the backyard and it was night, he was at least ready to be in a new time. A surprise but not a shock. It was annoying, but he was getting used to it. Lee guessed you could get used to a lot of things.

He looked around his backyard. It had to be fairly early. The lights in the houses across the back fence were still on—living rooms, kitchens, bedrooms. The traffic from nearby Irving and Lincoln streets was still pretty loud. He looked up at his house. His parents and whichever Lee this was tonight—older or younger— they were still awake, it seemed. Ten o'clock at the latest, his best guess.

"Sam?" he whispered to the backyard night. "Joan?"

This was new. Arriving in a new *when* without Sam and Joan. At least he was near his house.

But what about the guy who had been chasing him? Was he out here, ready to pounce?

"Dude?" Lee said to the night. Who was that guy?

Actually, Lee didn't need to ask. He knew who it was, it was just taking some time for the facts to stack up in his brain. It was all so . . . suddenly.

His pursuer was Lee himself, calling out, "Wait!" and chasing after him. Some older version of himself.

"Lee?" Lee called hoarsely to the night. "Me? Are you out there?"

He moved his feet, tested his arms. He seemed to be alone for now.

But which now? If only there were a newspaper stand in his backyard, then he could find out which now he'd suddenlied to.

Lee wanted to say it was November. The air was chilly—thanks again, Sam, for the jacket—and the night was darker and deeper than it would be if all those lights were on and it was still summer, say. It felt like the sun had set hours earlier.

And those clouds. Not fog—there was no fog at all. These few clouds seemed like the leftover clouds of a rainstorm. It could easily be November, when the rains returned.

Mostly, though, the night *smelled* like November. A deep autumn night. Crisp, shivery. There was a touch of wood smoke in the air, the clean scent of a recent rain, and below all that, the smell of summer's dead grasses and leaves. Not too long after Halloween. He was gonna call it . . . November 8th. His best guess.

Okay, that was two out of three: time of day, time of year. But which year?

The swing set in one corner of the yard looked almost haunted in the dark night. A skeleton swing set. All it needed was a little wind to drive one of the swings—Eek! eek!—to become creepy.

His *old* swing set. They'd gotten rid of it when he was ten. It was falling apart by then, and he was just too big for it. He remembered how sad he was when the junk guys took it away. Oh, well. So that would make tonight 2009 at the latest.

Lee moved towards the swing set. He was exposed in the open yard, but he also knew people didn't look out their windows at night. In all the lighted houses around him, most people were probably staring at some kind of a screen right now, TV or computer or phone. Too bad for them.

He sat down on a swing and stared up at his house. The lights were on in his parents' bedroom and in his own. He wondered if his younger self would come to the window and see his older self sitting on the swing set. But no one came to the window. He was probably watching TV.

Sticking out of the sandbox, which would eventually be taken away, too, Lee spotted one of his favorite toys of all time. He knew it the instant he saw it, and it almost made him laugh it made him so happy. A die-cast model of *Starcruiser Omega*.

Lee dropped into the sandbox pulled out the miniature spaceship, and blew the sand off of it. This was not his most expensive or his biggest or most complex toy. It was only about five inches long and crudely made, and it didn't do anything at all. But it fit perfectly into his hand, and he had loved to fly it around the galaxy and imagine the lives of the thousands of people in it. Whenever he'd watched *Starcruiser Omega* on TV with his dad, he held the toy in his lap.

He hadn't thought about this in ages.

One day, the *Starcruiser* disappeared. He never told his parents what had happened to it, even though he knew. Because he couldn't prove it. But he knew.

In third grade, Trevor McGahee had come over for a playdate. Lee's mom and Trevor's mom were friends back then, and they were always making the two of them play together. But even back then, Trevor was a goon. That day—Lee could see it all now—Trevor had come right out and asked Lee to give him the *Starcruiser*. Trevor wanted it. Lee said no, of course, but after Trevor left that day, Lee couldn't find the spaceship. He knew

Trevor had taken it, and he also knew he'd never get it back. Man, he loved that *Starcruiser*. He'd only had it a few months at the time.

If that was third grade, then this must be the autumn of—he counted backwards on his fingers—2007. The Lee Jones watching TV in that house was eight years old. Why had he left his *Starcruiser Omega* outside?

Night, autumn, 2007. Close enough for time travel. Lee's best guess. He'd got to where he wanted to be.

He raised the *Starcruiser* above his head and flew it through the vast reaches of space. Jumping, as they did in the show, from one corner of the universe to another. Just like Lee.

"Psst."

Lee certainly hoped it was Lee who'd just said "Psst" from the bushes in the corner of the yard. Because if it wasn't himself who'd just said "Psst," he thought he might actually freak out.

"Is that me?" Lee asked.

"Yes," said the voice from the bushes. "Is that me?"

"Yes, I'm me. Uh. We're me," thirteen-year-old Lee said.

Neither Lee moved. Lee figured Lee was nervous about meeting Lee.

"What do you want?" thirteen-year-old Lee asked.

"I have some things I want to tell you," Future Lee

said. "I thought you might have some questions about the future. I remembered that you—we—came to the house on this day. I remembered that we ended up here. It took me a while to get here. Sorry. For some reason, I ended up in the park on that last unstuck. In the Magic Forest."

The Magic Forest. Joan. Thirteen-year-old Lee had to pretend she was okay. Oh, he could ask. "Is Joan okay?"

"She's fine. Always has been."

"How old are you?" Lee asked.

"I'm fifteen," Future Lee said. "I was thinking about you today, and I remembered that I visited the house when I came unstuck that time with Sam, when I was thirteen, when I was you. Then I reached over to turn the stereo down, and zap, I got one of those static shocks, and there I was. In 2013. I was calling for you, and Joan and Sam were coming, but, pfft, you disappeared, and I did, too."

"Does this keep happening to us all the time?" thirteen-year-old Lee wanted to know. "I mean, coming unstuck?"

"No," Future Lee said. "Not to me, anyway. Not yet. I haven't come unstuck since the last time—"

"When was that?"

"It's been a while."

"So, I do get restuck in time again?"

"Yes."

"When?"

"Soon. Really, it's gonna be okay."

"Uh, you know, you can come out of the bushes now."

"Are we ready for this?" Future Lee asked.

"As we'll ever be."

Future Lee stepped out from behind the tangle of bushes. Thirteen-year-old Lee knew how he got there. There was a hole under the fence and, from there, a jagged path of holes under fences and gaps in other places, which took you on a journey through all the backyards between Eighth and Ninth Avenues. You could get all the way to Lincoln from here. Only kids knew about this, and they used the secret path all the time. The parents were clueless.

"Okay," Future Lee said. "Here goes."

He stepped out of the shadows.

Lee stood up and carefully regarded his future self.

Future Lee was decidedly taller. Quite a bit taller, six inches or so. This was a relief to Lee. In seventh and eighth grades, he had barely grown an inch, while all the girls, including Joan, had sprouted like dandelions. Lee thought he might be a shrimp forever. It was reassuring to be able to look up at himself.

There was no doubt that this boy was Future Lee.

The resemblance was remarkable. Lee still looked like himself, except a little older. This was something of a disappointment, though. He knew it was pure fantasy, but Lee often imagined future versions of himself—high school, college, beyond—that were radically different from the middle school Lee who looked back at him from the mirror each morning. The Future Lee that Lee had hoped for was more handsome with sharper features and had a body that was—magically—sculpted. Lee had hoped his future self would be a little less soft around the edges.

At least he was taller. A good start.

Oh, and his face was clear, no sign of acne yet. His hair was pretty cool, too. A little shorter but a little more, uh, shaped. It was a hairstyle not a haircut. Cool. And in the bright darkness of the city's night, Lee thought he might even have detected the hint of a mustache on his future self.

Clothes, pretty much the same. What did he expect? Lee figured you could go an entire lifetime in jeans and T-shirts. At least in San Francisco. You could even get by with that outfit in 1864. Then Lee realized that his future self was wearing a long-sleeved T-shirt under a short-sleeved T-shirt of some band called Quell Farm. His future look was pretty cool, a little rockier. Not bad. And, oh, where did he get those shoes? These were leather Kixes—pretty stylin'. Eighth-grade Lee would never have worn leather shoes, unless his mom made him. But tonight, on Future Lee, these shoes looked great. Lee would have to reconsider some things. Maybe it was time for a change.

The most surprising thing about Lee's meeting his future self in the backyard of his former self, was that it wasn't more surprising. Shouldn't his future self have a ray gun and a blue spandex suit and a robot dog? And shouldn't he be going on about saving mankind from destruction? You know, real time-travel-story stuff.

Future Lee was different, for sure, but he was also very much the same.

Future Lee held out his hand; Lee shook it.

"Pleased to meet me," they said in unison.

"Jinx," they both said.

"I guess we owe us a coke," Future Lee said.

And they both laughed, and that *was* kind of freaky, the exact same laughter erupting from two different bodies. This made them both laugh more, and they were both trying to stifle their laughter in their elbows, both bent over, laughing.

When they pulled it together, Lee straightened up and opened his eyes and asked his future self, "Why are you here?"

"I'm not sure," Future Lee said. They both moved to

the swing set, sat on swings, stared up at eight-year-old Lee's house. "I wasn't planning on this. But I'm here now. I must have wanted to tell you something."

They swung on the swings gently, without squeaking.

"And that would be?" Lee asked.

"Okay," Future Lee said. "You should know this. Sam was right. You cannot change the future by changing the past. I know that's why you're here—to change the future. Can't be done. There *is* only one river."

"How do you know?" Lee asked.

"I'm from the future? Duh."

"Oh. Right."

More swinging.

"But aren't you changing my future by coming here now?" Lee asked. "I mean, if you hadn't come, then—"

Future Lee stopped swinging. "See," he said, "that's the point. I *did* come. I *am* here now. There is no *if* about it. This is the *only* time this moment happens. Only and ever. No ifs. Did."

Lee was very confused by all this. But who wouldn't be?

He looked at Future Lee. He decided not to over-think this. It felt like it all made sense—in a time-travel way.

He got it. This was the only time he'd ever be here,

in this place, with this future self. Weird as it was to consider: This was simply the next moment in Lee's life. He figured he'd best make the most of it.

"Okay," Lee said. "I get it. But have you figured out why? Why this happens to us?"

Future Lee started to swing again.

"'Cause we're lucky," Future Lee said. "I've thought a lot about what Sam told us back then. I mean . . . *now*. I mean . . . *in the future*. Anyway. Some people are just lucky. They get to see more of time than other people. We do."

"That's it?" Lee asked himself.

"Pretty much. It just kind of happens."

"And?"

"I know. Let it sink in. It's going to take you—us—a while to get it. I'm still thinking about it. I can say this, though. Best thing about being unstuck is all the other unstuckers you meet. Sam, Gim, the misses. Joan."

Lee let this idea settle over him. He knew it was correct in some way, but he also knew it would take a very long time for it to make total sense.

"Can I ask a couple of questions?" Lee asked.

"A few," Future Lee said. "But you want the future to have some surprises."

"Joan?" he asked.

"She goes to Starr King, which kind of blows. But we're still best friends. No problem. And she's got this really cool friend, Camille. You'll like her."

"Mom and Dad?"

"Divorced. You'll live here with Mom. But you know what, it'll be okay. The first year sucks—hard. But after, it's not bad. You'll be amazed at how much happier everyone is."

Lee thought he would ask a whole bunch more questions—who would win the World Series this year, for instance—but all his questions came to rest. Nah. He could wait. He got it.

Long minutes passed. Swinging.

"Do you want to go inside?" Future Lee asked. "See who we were? I know it's why you came."

"What's the point?" Lee said. "To scare the pants off our eight-year-old self?"

"Right."

"Okay, future dude," Lee said. "Now what? How do we get out of here?"

"I have no freakin' idea," Future Lee said. "I just got here myself."

"Sam always said—"

"'Cast off,' that's what he always said," Future Lee said. "Let's pump these swings."

Lee figured that was as good an idea as any. But if it

worked . . . He hopped off the swing, went to the sand-box, pocketed the *Starcruiser*. He couldn't wait to show this to Trevor, couldn't wait to see the look on his face. Trevor would never figure out how Lee retrieved it. Plus, Lee would have it back. It probably wouldn't change any-thing, in the past or the future if Lee took it with him. It would still be there, he knew, for Trevor to steal. Lee knew this because he remembered it.

He hopped on a swing and joined his future self.

In seconds, the swings were squeaking, the whole swing set was creaking and swaying, and both Lees were rising high in the sky.

"Ready?" Future Lee called.

"Worth a shot."

"One, two, three!" they called together.

At the acme of his last ascent, going forward, Lee saw his past self come to the window of his past bedroom.

But it was too late to stop, too late even to wave. Lee's hands had let go of the chains, and he was flying up into the night sky.

He hoped wherever he landed was going to be soft.

SIXTEEN

A Cold Empty Wind – A Paper Anchor – A Future Worth Having – A Movie Moment – A Tingle and a Tumble

The only thing that kept Joan from falling apart was the letter she had written to herself from the future. She had been back at Gim's for over two hours, and Lee had not shown up yet. Lee had come unstuck first, and in a logical world, he should have been, therefore, the first to return. But Lee wasn't here.

At least, Sam was here. He had not come unstuck at all and had simply taken the N Judah back to Gim's to wait for them. He figured Joan and Lee would eventually end up back there.

Sam's hunch had only halfway come true, however. What should have been a "movie moment," Joan rushing into the shop, she and Lee reunited, was instead a moment of cold, empty wind in Joan's heart.

When she came into the shop, no one had to tell her Lee was not there; she felt his absence. She wanted to believe he was all right, that he was merely having some cool time adventure, and that they would be together again soon. But it was hard to believe what you could not see.

The only thing Joan had to hold on to was her letter, and while she told Gim and Sam everything that had happened to her, she clutched the letter with both hands, afraid to let it go. If something bad had happened to Lee, wouldn't her future self have told her about it?

Well, yes. Unless Lee had managed to get back to his past and somehow change that past. And by changing the past, had changed the future. And maybe those changes hadn't caught up with Joan's future self yet. That had been his plan all along, hadn't it?

God, Lee *was* a little rat! A *big* little rat! And she really missed him. It surprised her that she could be so angry with one person, while wanting nothing else in the world but to see that person. Joan held the letter in her lap, looking down at it. It was only paper, only marks on a page, but this message from her future self was all she had right now.

Gim's quiet smile seemed to see into the heart of

Joan's predicament. After he and Sam both read the letter, Gim continued to ask Joan about her future self, what she had seen in her future self, who she might be someday. His concern helped Joan believe Lee would come bursting into the herb shop any minute now.

Sam, however, was being annoying. He kept going on and on about Joan's car, the Prius Hybrid. He'd seen enough of the future to know that automobiles would one day conquer the planet, and enough of that future, too, to know how much damage they would do.

"Imagine that," he said, "by inventing the hybrid car, you could do a good thing for our poor beleaguered world *and* make a fortune, too. Tell me more of this Pray-us, Joan."

"Pree-us," she said.

Joan, clutching the letter, kept trying to get back to talk of her future self and what the heck to do about Lee. Finally, she and Gim just ignored Sam and continued to talk about the future.

Sam hardly noticed. He was busy making notes and diagrams on a torn bit of brown paper bag. He used one of Gim's Bic pens—"Gim Chang's Herb and Ginger, Chinatown's Oldest and Finest"—to draw and write with, exclaiming now and then that this self-contained pen with no need for an inkwell was another marvel of the future.

"You said before," Joan said to Gim, "that you had met your future self. What was that like?"

"Yes," he said. "I've had the pleasure a few times. But that first time was the most important. You see, when I was twelve, my father died quite suddenly. A heart attack. He was my best friend, and I loved him very much. Two days after his funeral, I came unstuck for the first time. I could not imagine a future without him, you see."

Gim looked away from Joan, as if this wound still pained him. He shook his head a little, then folded his hands on the table.

"On my second or third unstuck," he went on, "I ran into myself. Or should I say, my older self found me. That Gim was around Sam's age now, twenty-eight or so. He had come looking for me in a time neither of us shared. He came up to me at a street corner in 1898, but I recognized him right away. I was pretty freaked out by his appearance, I have to say, but I was pretty freaked out already."

Joan thumbed the letter.

"He had a simple message for me. He wanted me to know that my family and our herb shop would survive my father's death, and that, all in all, everything would be okay. He also wanted me to know that I would never get over my father's death, that my father would stay with me every day of my life. This, he told me, was a good thing."

Gim smiled at Joan, clear and bright.

"And then," he said, "he simply evaporated. Right before my eyes. My future self had only that simple message, but it was crucial to me. I still miss my father, every single day, but the future, it turned out, was inevitable and worth believing in. Shortly after he disappeared, I came restuck in my own time and allowed the future to proceed."

Sam was still doodling, but he was edging away from Gim and Joan, turning his back on them. But while Gim told his story, Sam kept sheepishly looking over at them.

Joan knew a NO LOOK when she saw one. What was he hiding?

"Gim," Joan said boldly. "You say your future self came looking for you, the way mine came looking for me?"

"Yes." There was his wicked smile again.

"And that your future self just 'evaporated'?"

"Yes."

"The way that mysterious stranger—the one who followed us here—keeps evaporating?"

"Very much the same," Gim said. His smile grew that much more sly.

"Sam," Joan called.

The Bic pen clattered to the floor.

"Didn't you say you've never met your future self?"

"I do believe," Sam said, "I may have said that." He began to fold the paper bag into tinier and tinier squares.

"I wonder why that is," Gim said.

Joan knew she and Gim were on the same page. They looked at each other and were all like, GOT HIM.

"Sam," Joan said. "I think I know who that stranger is. And I think *you* know, too."

Sam couldn't help but look at Joan. His head was on a string, and Joan had tugged it. WHO ME? his LOOK said.

"I think," Joan said, "the mysterious stranger is—"

And, of course, that's when Lee came bursting into the shop. He was sweaty and jangly and saying something about the mysterious stranger.

But there was no time for any of that. First, it was movie-moment time.

Joan raced across the backroom to hug Lee. Embarrassing, yes, but she couldn't help herself. Leap, run, hug.

"You're back, you're back," she was saying, jumping up and down and still hugging.

"I'm back, I'm back," Lee said. He broke from the hug but did not let go of Joan. He held her shoulders, looked straight into her eyes, and they were both going, PHEW.

Joan was too happy to be mad at him. She'd save that for later—the little rat.

Sam slapped Lee on the shoulder. Gim smiled warmly.

Joan and Lee had to look at each other for a few more moments.

Then Lee was all, "Mysterious stranger this, mysterious stranger that," and Joan and Sam were tossing questions left and right, the backroom of the herb shop a-riot with noise.

"Stop!" Lee chased away the noise with this one word. Joan looked at him again. Wherever—*whenever*—he'd been, something had changed. He was so . . . urgent.

"Sorry," he said, "but this is important. Sam, I know who the mysterious stranger is. It's you, Sam, your future self. It's Mark Twain. Isn't it?"

Everyone turned to Sam, who was too struck to look away. And too stunned to speak.

Joan turned to Lee. She herself had been on the verge of saying the exact same thing, in fact, had been halfway through that sentence when Lee burst in. She had put several separate ideas together and had come up with the same notion as Lee had just done. The mysterious stranger in black who'd been tracking them was no less than Mark Twain, the person Sam Clemens would one day be. Sam's future self. But Lee beat her to it.

Normally, being beaten to the solution of any

problem would cause Joan both grief and rage. Not today. Lee had said it first. Good for him.

"Yeah, Sam," Joan said. "Lee's right, isn't he?"

Gim barked a laugh.

"What are you speaking of?" Sam said, giving them a rather feeble NO LOOK.

"Fine," Lee said. "Let me explain," and he was off with his story. He told about ending up in the backyard in his past and the *Starcruiser Omega* and meeting his future self and his cool new haircut and how he and Joan were still friends and how weird and wonderful it had been.

Joan was so relieved. She had hoped through the weirdness of everything that Lee would meet his future self, too. She had loved meeting her own future self, had needed it. She had wanted the same for Lee.

She and Lee looked at each other. NO FREAKIN' WAY. But back to Sam.

Lee had landed in the Broadway tunnel, just west of Chinatown. He figured—it *felt* like—he was in 2013 again, so he set off for Gim's. But there, on the opposite pedestrian walkway, was the mysterious stranger in black, calling out to him, and this time he called him by name.

"Lee, Lee," the stranger called. "Don't you remember me? We've got to talk about Sam."

Too many weirdnesses there. The butchers had called out for Twain, not Sam. So this was no butcher. How would a butcher know Lee's name, and why the whole "remember me?" bit.

Then it hit Lee. Sam had not met his future self and always got a little squirrelly whenever he talked about Twain. Gim had met his future self, Lee had, and now he knew Joan had, too. Who else could the stranger have been? Who else would be coming unstuck and following Sam through time?

Lee continued his story. He had stopped in the tunnel, no longer afraid, and called out, "Mark Twain, is that you?" What a crazy thing to be calling out in 2013.

The stranger waved again, opened his mouth to speak, then—pfft!—was gone. Unstuck again. No doubt about it.

"I was just gonna say the same thing," Joan said. She did want to go on record.

Lee: SU-URE. Joan: REALLY. Together: COOL.

All eyes back to Sam.

"Sam?" Gim said.

They were all standing. This was no sit-down, green tea and almond cookies discussion.

"I recollect," Sam said, "a stretch of trail just west of Saint Louis where—"

"Sam," Lee said. "Seriously."

"And in that country," Sam said, "the rabbits are bigger than—"

"Sam." Joan was all serious.

"A man I knew," Sam said, "managed to saddle one of those rabbits and—"

"Sam," Gim said with gentle gravity. "Talk to them."

Sam sighed, deflated. He leaned on his fists on the table. "I believe you are correct," he said. "The both of you. I have thought for some time it must be this Twain fellow I've heard so much about. He has haunted me for weeks. But I've no wish to speak with him."

Joan saw something low and dark in Sam's eyes.

"Why are you afraid of him?" she asked.

Sam was shocked—or tried to appear to be.

"Yes," Joan said, "afraid. Why not talk to him? We've all spoken to our future selves. We liked it; it helps."

Sam paced in a circle, fingering his pipe.

"I am not yet convinced," he said, "that I am capable of the greatness that's been ascribed to me. What if I am not worthy? Look at me, a young reporter, with only one thin dime and a hundred dollar gold piece to my name. I live in an abandoned, un-seaworthy ship, and the one thing I've written worth writing—the story of the butchers and their Chinese victim—I cannot get published. What would this Twain fellow say to me?"

Joan turned to Gim. She wanted him to step in. But Gim shrugged and passed the duty back to Joan.

"He would tell you," Joan said, "that you must try. That you should *cast off*."

Sam would not look at Joan.

"I am afraid to even try," he said.

It was strange to see Sam this way, all the brash taken out of him. Deflated. But oddly reassuring, too. It made Sam seem more real.

"I am afraid of trying," Sam said, "because I want so badly to be who I think I might one day be. And if I fail . . . I'll have no future at all."

"You're being stupid," Lee said. Mr. Diplomacy.

"At least talk to Twain," Joan said.

"I prefer not to," Sam said.

"Sam Clemens—" Joan was winding up to give Sam another big speech, but at that moment there was a loud pounding on the shop's front door and a voice calling out for Sam. The stranger.

In the quiet of the shop's backroom, Joan clearly heard the voice, a honey-rich drawl that was surely an older version of Sam's.

Sam looked once towards the front of the shop, then turned and bolted out the back door into the small courtyard.

Without a LOOK, without a word, without a second

thought, Lee and Joan took off after Sam. Joan grabbed the soldier's backpack but stopped for one second to call out to Gim. "*Sheh-sheh. Yat lou ping on.*" Would she ever see him again?

Sam had disappeared through the back door of a shop across the courtyard, but Lee was close behind. Joan turned on her booster rockets and soon was right behind Lee, zipping down an aisle of green plastic Buddhas and Kwan Yins and waving lucky cats and cheap gaudy tea sets.

They came out of the souvenir store on Grant, but Sam, it turned out, could motor, too. He was far ahead, turning another corner. Joan flipped on the hyper-booster rockets and zoomed past Lee, gaining on Sam. But Lee had some kind of bonus points he'd been saving, and he stayed right behind her, keeping pace. Who knew the boy could run so fast?

It was evening now, still foggy, a brutally cold fog that whipped down the streets on sharp bursts of wind. Joan was determined not to lose Sam in the fog or the Chinatown crowds.

Sam turned down an alley, but he was slowing, and they were speeding, and in a few strides, Joan caught his coattails and tried to slow him down, calling softly, breathlessly, "Sam, Sam, it's okay." Lee grabbed Joan's jacket, and they all shuddered to a halt.

The sun, surprisingly, broke through the fog to reveal a big patch of bright blue sky. What a weird place San Francisco was, Joan thought. Fog in the summer, cold and gray, then, oops, here's a perfectly sunny day.

Should it be daytime, though? Wasn't it evening? There was a tingling sensation in Joan's arms and legs, and she knew it wasn't from running. This was something else, something new.

All three looked up at the bright patch of clear sky, and so did not see the four-horse carriage that thundered towards them.

Horses, carriage, sun. Unstuck again, Joan realized.

Before she could figure *when* they were, Lee was pushing her and Sam away from the flashing hooves of the carriage horses, and they all fell to the rubbery sidewalk.

The orange sodium lights above her were bright in Joan's eyes, the sidewalk soft beneath her. It was night, she knew, but all the lights made a day-night of the sky. It was hard to see where she was. And the sirens that pierced the city's din made it hard to concentrate.

Unstuck, then unstuck again.

Where were they? Not 1864. Not 2013, not 2012.

What was that up in the sky?

Joan put her hands flat on the ground. Wished there were some kind of handle there.

"Do you two," Sam said, "remember me talking about

tumblin'? Well, you might want to hold on. I do believe we have started to tumble."

The Coca-Cola advertising satellite rose high into the night, bright red and white, as big as a full moon over whichever San Francisco this was.

SEVENTEEN

Tumble – Tumble Again – Wait! Is That? – Nope, Still Tumblin' – Keep Them Dogies Tumblin'

This was one of those moments, Lee knew, when it was best to stand still. When life got a little too woogata-woogata, a little too fast and furious. Sometimes it was smart to be still and let the world spin around you.

Sam seemed to agree with Lee's strategy: Be still. Both he and Joan were playing that super-number-one-fun-time-game, Who Can Stand Stillest.

When they'd turned the corner and the horses and carriage were suddenly on top of them, Lee was okay with that, even with the approaching danger. Weird as it was, Lee was getting used to finding himself in another time. But usually he stayed in that time, at least for a while. This time they'd come unstuck again right away and found themselves in a *when* Lee could only think of as the Way Future.

Lee looked around. Yep. Capital *F* Future. Jetpack Future.

The dead giveaway was the enormous Coke advertisement. Round and red, with the familiar white lettering, the ad hung far above the city, a shining second moon. The ad wasn't hung on the bottom of a blimp, though, or strung from the back of an airplane. The Coke ad was much higher in the sky. In fact, it wasn't *in* the sky, per se, it was *above* the sky. It was in space. Way far up there. And there, rising behind the skyscraper skyline, was the Golden Arches moon. The other moon, the real moon, wasn't visible.

Whoa. What a weird future they'd landed in, where two of the three moons were satellite advertisements for junk food.

Lee stayed still. The only thing stiller than Lee was Joan.

Finally, he spoke out of the stillness.

"So, Sam," Lee said, "you've done this before?"

"Yep," Sam said.

"So, uh," Lee said. "I'm gonna stand real still. Sound good to you?"

"Solid plan, dude," Sam said. "I'm all for standing still. I found it works wonders. During a tumble, at least. To the best of my ability to know such things, I believe we cannot be seen right now. If that helps you at all."

They were on the sidewalk of a very busy street. Cars and trucks, all covered in flashing lights, zoomed by. Crowds of city dwellers—some of them in neon-lighted hats—flowed around the three Unstuckians.

"You see," Sam said. "It's my theory from my own limited experience that when we're tumblin', really moving and falling through time, we're in a kind of bubble, a pocket. We're not really in any time at all right now. Just passing through."

Lee was willing to buy that theory. Even though the ground under his feet wasn't particularly solid. In the future, it seemed, sidewalks were softer, like that stuff in playgrounds.

Joan seemed to be listening, but she did not move.

"Any idea how long we'll be here?" Lee asked.

"Not a one," Sam said.

"Joan?" Lee said into the night. "You still there?"

"I'm here," she said. And she said it very loudly. But no one from the future noticed her.

"You okay?" Lee asked.

"I'm good," she yelled. "You know, just getting my sea legs. Uh, *time* legs."

"You hear what Sam said?"

"Roger. Copy that. I'm good with standing still."

The street where they stood looked more like Tokyo than San Francisco. At least, some movie version of Tokyo. It was all skyscrapers and flashing-light advertisements and shops selling all sorts of gizmos that flashed and beeped.

A lot of the signs were in English, a whole bunch in Chinese. Some were in Spanish, some in Russian and Japanese, some were in languages Lee didn't recognize at all. Some of the signs seemed to be a combination of all languages.

A MUNI train hissed to a stop right in front of them. Well, it said MUNI on the side, in the same tubular letters Lee was used to. But this MUNI train was a double-decker, and instead of two cars long, it was at least eight. The digital advertisements that covered the train cars morphed continually from one product to another—cameras, phones, cars, hamburgers.

The doors of the MUNI cars opened, and the packed mob of passengers poured out. An amplified voice, a woman's, filled the air. "Eighth Avenue and Irving, Eighth Avenue and Irving. Mind the doors." The doors pulled shut with a thwock, and the N Judah—it was an N Judah, Lee saw now—squealed down the tracks. No matter how far into the future this was, MUNI still hadn't developed a train that didn't squeal.

Joan reached across Sam to squeeze Lee's hand, and in that wordless gesture, she made him pay attention to the words he ought to have been paying attention to.

"Eighth Avenue and Irving."

This was *his* MUNI stop. *His* corner. Which meant that *his* house was now a skyscraper office building. He couldn't see the top of the building, lost as it was in the bright lights of the future.

It wasn't that Lee couldn't move or didn't want to move towards where his "old" house used to be. He simply didn't move. If he took one step, he might enter the future in a more permanent way.

Lee wasn't bothered by the absence of his house. That, he figured, was to be expected. Heck, he realized, he might be an old, old man in this future, or even long dead.

No, what bothered Lee most were the cars. Here he was, way into the future, and people were still driving cars. The streets were packed with them—gasoline-powered cars, you could tell by the sound and smell. Time continued to pass, the future continued to arrive, but humans were still ruining the planet.

He looked over at Joan. She was smiling again. A good sign.

"Sam," Joan said. "Do you have any idea *when* this is?"

"All I can tell you is it's Thursday," Sam said.

He pointed to a large screen that occupied an entire wall of a building across Irving. Big words flashed over and over on the screen—"Today is Thursday!"

A troop of police helicopters thudded over Eighth Avenue.

"Sam," Lee said. "What do we do?"

"Let's just wait a minute," Sam said. "I've got this feeling."

"Oh, good," Joan said. "A feeling. You know, a fact can be just as good as a feeling sometimes."

Sam laughed. Lee felt a tingling in his arms and legs, the same feeling he'd had before the tumble started, like tiny fish swimming in his veins.

The facade of the building across from them lit up with brilliant white lights, which swirled and cascaded, pinwheeling over the building, forming words and phrases that must be an advertisement, although it was unclear what was being advertised.

"Everything Must Go," the building said.

"Today Is Thursday," it said.

"The Time Is Now," it said.

And when the word "Now" appeared on the building, every light in the display went supernova white. It was blinding.

Lee couldn't see a thing. He heard Joan go, "Oooooh."

When his eyesight returned, Lee figured, they would probably find themselves in a different *when*. He was getting a feel for tumblin'.

True enough. The white lights of the building's advertisement dimmed in his eyes, and Lee saw that they were no longer in a city. There was instead, not far off, the dim orange blur of a campfire. Lee thought he heard the sound of singing.

They were near the bay—Lee could smell it. And it was cold. Really cold.

Around the large campfire, a ring of people were gathered, scores of them. Strings of children weaved in and out of the circle of light, chasing one another. Beyond this ring were several cone-shaped huts.

Lee looked at Joan and Sam. Their faces flickered in the dim light of the fire; their mouths hung open. Lee suspected his own mouth was hanging open, too. They were obviously no longer in the future. This was an Indian village.

The moon was full tonight—whatever night this was—and there were no advertising satellites to compete with it. The moon, bright blue, hung over the earth and threw crisp blue shadows on the ground. Sheets of blue light covered the waters of the bay. Lee thought he could see forever under this moon. There, to the east, was Mount Diablo. Where it always was.

The singing from the fireside flowed over Lee. The music, the sound of human voices together, was so strange and so beautiful at the same time he couldn't move if he wanted to.

"Ohlone," Joan said. "This is an Ohlone village. They used to live here. Once the Gold Rush started, they didn't last very long. I did a report in sixth grade."

Leave it to Joan. Was there any topic she had not done a report on? Lee could only imagine how many extra-credit points she had banked.

"I believe you are correct," Sam said.

"Their huts are made of tule reeds," Joan said. "They also make canoes that way. But now the reeds are gone, and we can only imagine how they lived. This whole world, it's gone."

"Gone?" Sam asked.

"Practically."

"That's a shame," Sam said. "I always liked the Ohlone. Met many of them in San Francisco. Very kind, very funny, and not one of 'em ever once tried to sell me a surefire gold mine."

"What are they singing?" Lee asked. "It's beautiful."

The crowd drew closer to the fire and to one another. Even the children left off their games and huddled next to their parents. Waves of song rose into the night.

"My guess," Sam said, "is that they are singing about what people have been singing about since we could sing. Maybe why we started singing in the first place. They're probably thanking the universe for the day that just ended and wondering at the same time if the universe would be so kind as to send them another day. Like most of us, they just want to know that the sun will rise again."

The last notes of the song faded.

Children broke away from their parents, picked up their games. The adults chatted and tidied up. This was the last hour of the day.

"Sam," Lee said. "Maybe it's 1864, maybe you're home."

"I thought so, too, at first," Sam said. "But look, there's where downtown should be."

They were very close to where the *Paul Jones* was marooned, but there was only hillside, marshland, and bay. Whenever this was, the Gold Rush had not yet occurred.

"So we could be any time," Joan said. "Could be two hundred years ago, five hundred."

"Yep," Sam said. What was it that was so reassuring about Sam's "Yep"? His "Yep" never changed anything;

it only accepted the obvious. Whenever Sam said yep, Lee felt better.

"Wow." What else could Lee say?

Somewhere not far behind them, a dry twig snapped. Lee turned to see what creature approached; he suspected it was the stranger. Sam and Joan were turning, too, and Lee figured that when they stopped turning, they would no longer be near the Ohlone village. At least, not near it in time.

Tumbled again.

It was hard to say if this new *when* was day or night. No moon. It was dark, that much was certain, the sky black and gray and every combination of those colors. Dark as the sky was, though, it seemed to be on fire.

The sharp tang in the air caught in Lee's nose and throat. The sky was burning.

Where they stood, Lee reckoned, was where they had been standing just a moment before—near the bay. But they'd obviously tumbled forward again in time.

There was downtown San Francisco, all ablaze, its buildings cracked and ruined, black clouds erupting from the earth. And all around the perimeter of downtown, crowds of citizens circled the inferno, like kids at a concert.

An incessant clanging of bells, the rumble of the fire itself.

No one said anything; no one had to. Lee knew *exactly* when this was.

It was April 18, 1906. The Great Earthquake.

"Oh, my Lord," Sam said. "I've heard about this, even saw some photographs, but nothing could . . ."

Sam stopped talking. Lee and Joan couldn't even get started.

They watched the city burn.

Lee stole a glance at Joan. Had they run out of LOOKS?

That tingling again.

"Hold on," Sam said. "I believe we're about to pick up speed. Been on this stretch of the river before."

"Riders," Lee said, "please keep your arms and legs inside the space-time continuum at all times. And we do mean all times."

Joan hiccupped a laugh, then uttered a tiny little "Oh."

Without a blink or trip or jerk or fall or step or turn, the scene changed again.

The black burning sky gave way to cloudy twilight. Big clouds caught the orange-and-pink glow of the setting sun.

The Bay Bridge was there again, but the Transamerica Pyramid wasn't, and downtown was shorter than in Lee's time.

It was chilly and the air was still, but the city was far from quiet. The waterfront was a zoo of ships along the docks and on the bay. The sky was a rush hour—planes of all sizes, propeller planes, all flying west, towards the Pacific.

"War," Joan said. "It's World War Two. Oh, my God."

And it was, the only explanation. Even Lee had done a report on World War Two.

"The big war?" Sam asked. "In the 1940s? With Germany and Japan?"

"That's the one," Joan said.

"Oh," was all Sam could muster.

Lee desperately wanted to say something, but nothing would come. Now he understood the true meaning of the phrase *too much information*. He couldn't even say wow.

The scene changed again. And again. And again. It was like being at one of those IMAX planetarium shows, where you watch a movie, but your body *feels* the sailing or soaring or diving. Only this theater was run by a crazy person. Mad IMAX, Lee thought, and then he thought, Hey, that's pretty funny. He'd have to remember that one.

The scene changed constantly—bam! bam! bam! The weather changed; the time of day changed. The city grew, shrank, fell over, rose again, disappeared. It was clear they were jumping up and down in time, back and forth. Randomly?

At one point, Lee thought he saw a trail of Spanish soldiers nearby; and another time, a ruined city buried under sand and grass and trees.

Sam had taken Lee's hand, and he knew from the way they all stood that he had taken Joan's hand, too.

It might have been an IMAX show, or it might have been a dream—it might even have been a really good book. But this was no illusion. Everything Lee saw around him changed and changed. Except the one place where he stood.

Lee could not look at his fellow travelers; he wanted to see everything.

The tumble seemed to slow for a moment. They were still in San Francisco but terribly alone. Under a stunning blue sky, a pristine bay. The nearby hills were slightly altered, the bay's shoreline quite different, and some of the trees and plants were unfamiliar.

This San Francisco showed no trace of humans.

"So," Lee said. "Do we think this is before humans arrived? Or after they left?"

Whether before or after humans, this was clearly the farthest Lee had been from home. A shiver ran through him. What if they were stranded?

An enormous black condor swooped low over their

heads. The bay glittered under the warm sun. Oh, well. There were worse *whens* to be stranded in.

Behind them a twig snapped again.

"Sam," the stranger's voice called.

Sam rushed ahead, away from the voice, pulling Lee and Joan with him.

Ow, that hurt. Oh, unstuck again.

But the tingling was gone now, and there, around the curve of the bay, was the Street of Ships and, beyond, the green gaslight glow of San Francisco. They were home. Well, Sam was home.

Joan and Lee looked at each other.

He wondered if they had run out of LOOKS. But there appeared to be one more LOOK, one that was deeper and more complex than any other had ever been.

I CAN'T BELIEVE THIS—THAT WAS AWESOME—I MEAN, DID YOU SEE THAT? IT WAS AWESOME, AND I GET IT. YOU GET IT. I NEVER KNEW THIS WHOLE TIME THING, TIME AS A RIVER, IT'S BIGGER THAN WE ARE. IT'S HUGE, AND IT'S UP TO US TO FIGURE OUT HOW WE FIT IN—

EIGHTEEN

There We Go Again – The Golden West – A Glorious Sleep – A Knock on the Door

—IT'S NOT ABOUT MAKING THE FUTURE FIT US, AND IT'S WEIRD BECAUSE THAT'S A GOOD THING, NOT A HORRIBLE THING, AND I WOULDN'T CHANGE ANYTHING WE'VE SEEN, AND I'M PRETTY SURE WE'LL GET HOME, BUT FIRST WHAT ARE WE GOING TO DO ABOUT SAM? WE HAVE TO HELP HIM. MAN, THAT WAS AWESOME.

This was the BEST LOOK EVER that Joan had shared with Lee.

The shimmering sensation that had run up and down Joan's arms and legs during the tumble was gone.

"Home again, home again," Sam said.

"Jiggety-jig," Lee said.

"We're done tumblin', aren't we?" Joan asked.

"Yep," was all Sam needed to say.

From their spot on Mission Bay, where they'd dizzily swirled through so many *whens*, Joan could clearly see the Street of Ships. This was, without a doubt, 1864— Joan remembered it. The night was warm and still, exactly as it had been the night they'd left. She remembered *everything*.

Yes, home again. Well, home of a sort.

Joan could almost feel the scratchy wool blankets of the bed on the *Paul Jones*, could definitely feel the tug of sleep. She was so tired. How long had they been awake? Too many days had happened in this one day for Joan to be able to count hours.

"There," Lee shouted, and he ran forward, pointing. "It's the *Paul Jones*. We're ho—"

But the word "home" was cut off by the explosion that shook the *Paul Jones*. Joan recognized the sound. Not the type of sound, mind you, but the exact sound. She'd heard it the last time she was in 1864.

Flames shot up out of the *Paul Jones*, and a chorus of voices erupted from that direction. The butchers had set fire to the ship—again.

It was 1864. That night. That hour.

Neither Sam nor Lee nor Joan moved.

Lee said, "Hey," and the minute Joan heard that "Hey," she knew what would follow.

If they had returned to 1864 and the night the butchers burned the *Paul Jones*—and they most certainly had—then right about now, a small sailboat should be . . .

"Shouldn't we—" Lee said. Two shotgun blasts rang out. "Yes, yes, there we are."

The boat's white sail billowed and caught on the breeze, and it tacked away from shore. Three dark shapes rode low in the boat—Sam and Lee and Joan herself. A Joan from two days before.

It made sense, a bit, that if you could see your future self getting into a car and driving off, then you should also be able to see your past self. Joan found it a little troubling, though, that this past self was so recent. If she could catch up with that self of hers, the one riding out on the dark waters, what would she say?

Have fun. Look around. It'll be okay.

"Look at us go," Lee said.

The Street of Ships erupted, shouts and bells filling the air. Fire wagons rattled into view. The *Paul Jones* was fully engulfed.

Sam said nothing, always an unusual occurrence. Joan tore her gaze from the fire to find Sam looking about nervously.

Joan looked about, too. No mysterious stranger.

Sam looked miserable, shaken.

"Well, now," he said, "with the *Paul Jones* ablaze, we'd best find another place to stow away. I say we roust out Smiggy and see if that chucklehead—"

Sam started to walk away, but Joan set herself directly in his path, which was enough to stop his speech. Joan's expression at that moment was fierce enough to stop a locomotive. Lee stood right next to her, the gaze he aimed at Sam as fierce as her own. NUFF SAID.

"Stop," Joan said. "You cannot keep running from your future. You say, 'Ohhhhhh, I wanna be a great writer, see everything in the whole world,' but then, no, you chicken out. It's really kind of embarrassing, don't you think?"

"Yeah," Lee said. "What she said."

"But I—"

"But what?" Joan was on a roll now. "You're all, 'Cast off, brave sailors,' then you run? You know you're going to be Mark Twain. You *know* it. Stop trying to paddle upstream."

Lee looked at Joan. GOOD ONE.

Sam's shoulders fell. Then he pulled himself up straight, breathed in deeply. GRATITUDE.

"True enough," Sam said. "But what should I do? Stand here and wait?"

Lee hopped on that one. "Didn't you say you had an 'official residence'?" Lee was still trying to look fierce, but his goofy grin was starting to creep back in. "Some hotel? I like the sound of that, a hotel."

"Yes," Sam said, "the Golden West. But how will Twain know to find me there?"

"Because he'll remember," Joan said. "*You'll* remember where you went to wait for him. I mean, wait for you."

All three shared a LOOK. CAST OFF.

The Golden West Hotel, at the corner of Market and Powell, smack in the heart of downtown, was quite a bit fancier than Joan had envisioned. The lobby was all marble and carved wood and gilt decorations, and the ceiling must have been three stories high. The lobby's red velour sofas were overshadowed by full-size palm trees in enormous planters. Two stuffed grizzly bears engaged in ferocious battle occupied the lobby's vast space.

San Francisco in 1864 was both rich and poor, fancy and rugged. Just like every other San Francisco Joan had ever seen, including her own.

Joan retrieved the slouch hat from the backpack,

and as they approached the front desk, pulled it down far over her face again. No need to be foolish, even though she felt much less afraid in this *when* than she had before.

The butchers, she knew, were busy running from the fire. And having seen the future, and how the Chinese in San Francisco had overcome so much, Joan felt an extra jolt of courage.

The desk clerk, in a red velvet suit with gold epaulets, popped up from behind the counter, looking as if he'd never been happier to see anyone.

"Mr. Twain, sir," he squealed. "Good evening. It has been too long an absence, sir. I imagine that you and your reportorial skills have been out searching the hinterlands of our great state for a bounty of journalistic inspiration, no?"

From a grid of pigeonholes behind him, the clerk pulled out a room key, presenting it to Sam as if it were made of the rarest jewels.

"Evenin', Bascom, no need to lasso the calf you already caught, now is there?" Sam tipped his hat.

"Your guests, sir? May I offer them a room as well?"

"We're fine," Sam said. "My nephews will stay in my suite." Joan had forgotten she was dressed as a boy. "But we are hungry as a herd of heifers. Kitchen open?"

"Sir, yes, sir."

The next thing, they were on the third floor in the living room of a suite as opulent as the lobby and nearly as spacious.

"Courtesy of the *Morning Call*," Sam said. "Though why a reporter should deserve such amenities eludes me to this day. I suppose the editors offer such posh accommodations to keep us beholden to them. For most reporters, a desk to sleep under would suffice."

A bellboy brought their suppers, and without a word, they loaded up their plates and dug ferociously into cold chicken and potato salad. Oh, my God, it was good.

Then they talked.

They could finally talk.

They tried, as a team, to count how many *whens* they had passed through on their tumble and agreed there had been too many to count. They did what you have to do after an adventure of such size—they went over every detail, again and again.

Yes, Joan had to agree with Lee and Sam. The tumble had been exhilarating and terrifying and totally awesome, and none of them would trade it for all the world.

Then Joan told Lee about her future self and showed him the note she had written to herself and showed him, too, the Heartless book she'd bought. She gave Sam and Lee their bookmarks.

But she didn't forget to give Lee a hard time for leaving her on her own like that. Though she was no longer angry with him, she felt she owed him a little grief nonetheless.

Lee told them in more detail about his past house and his future self, and showed them the *Starcruiser Omega* he had retrieved. Sam was quite taken with Lee's toy, the detail, the solidity of it, the idea of space flight.

"Why, when I was a lad," he said, "my only toys were old chicken bones, maybe a piece of string if I was lucky."

The best discovery was that Joan and Lee knew they would remain best friends; they had told themselves that.

Joan took Lee's hand and held it tight.

Sam had the decency to look away.

Then the fatigue bore down on Joan, nearly swept her away at the table. She moved to one of the sofas and lay down. Lee and Sam continued talking, and Joan struggled to keep her eyes closed but still stay awake. She drifted in and out.

Lying there, she recalled that first night on the *Paul Jones*, crammed into those tight quarters, afraid, hopeless. Here, in this opulent hotel room, safe with friends, this was much better. She wasn't home yet, but neither was she homeless. She had her traveling companions.

. . .

When Joan woke, it was still the Golden West, still 1864. But morning now. Just your average passing of time.

And she was still on the sofa, a blanket placed over her. Was this the most comfortable sofa ever or what? With the sun streaming in the hotel windows, Joan snuggled deeply into the cushions.

She thought about her home—her 2012 home—and how nice it would be to get back there, to see her family again, to get restuck. But she could wait. First, there was Sam to take care of.

Sam! The stranger!

She sat up.

Sam and Lee stood by one of the high windows, while Sam directed Lee's gaze over the Market Street scene. A steam train blew its thunderous, deep call. Good, Sam was still here.

The knock on the door was insistent but not impatient.

Sam reached for his derringer.

Joan would have none of that.

"What? You're gonna shoot yourself?" Then she called out, all breezy and light, "Who is it?"

"Sam," the voice said. "I'm looking for Sam Clemens.

C'mon, Sam, I know you're in there. I'd like to speak with you."

"Who are you?" Sam asked. He moved to the door, put one hand on it.

"It's me, Sam," the voice said. "Which is you, of course. Mark Twain."

"How did you know I was here?"

"I remembered," Twain said. "I remembered coming here with Joan and Lee. It's one of the great adventures of our life. Though not the last."

Sam said nothing.

Sam looked at Lee and Joan, who looked back at him. JUST DO IT.

Sam opened the door.

The mysterious stranger was dressed all in black like Sam. But when he removed his black slouch hat, there was the all too famous Mark Twain shock of white hair and unmistakable white mustache.

"It's about time," Twain said.

There was no doubt this was Mark Twain, Sam's future self.

Sam and Twain shook hands.

That was weird, Joan thought, and very cool. Lee was pretty much dancing.

"Lee, Joan," Twain said. "It's so very good to see you again."

They each shook hands with Twain.

"May I come in?" he asked. "Can we talk, Sam? I don't have much time."

Joan was just staring. It was strange to see the young Sam and the old Twain looking at each other. But most impressive was the simple fact that this was Mark Twain, the famous writer. Wow. She'd definitely have to do a report about this. Would it be rude to ask for an autograph?

Sam, unable to speak, gestured for Twain to move to one of the sofas. They sat on either end.

"Hey," Lee blurted. "If you're Mark Twain, where's your white suit? You always wear a white suit."

"Oh, ho," Twain said. "You mean my don't-care-a-damn suit, all white linen and scarlet socks? My Mark Twain suit? I only wear that when I'm playing at Mark Twain. I'm always—always!—Sam Clemens deep down. And do you know how hard it is to keep a white suit clean? Especially when you smoke a cigar. I switched to cigars some years back, Sam, when I came into money at last."

Joan and Lee sat on the facing sofa, perched on the edge of it.

Twain pulled out a cigar and lit it; Sam retrieved and lit his pipe. Same but different.

Normally Joan would have gone ballistic, made

them go outside to smoke. But this was a special occasion.

Sam and Twain puffed up clouds of smoke. Stared at each other.

"What do you want?" Sam said.

"Well," Twain said, puffing up more cloud—he puffed exactly like Sam. "I know you're worried right now. And I want to tell you not to be. Ever since those dastardly butchers, you've been wondering if you should stop all this newspaper foolishness. If you should aim for something else. Something that will last longer. Dare I say it? Literature."

"Yes. That is true."

"It seems as if you know it. But you aren't sure you can do it. To be blunt, my friend, you don't know if you've got stories to tell. Important stories."

"I don't know where to start," Sam said. "You've done so much. Everyone says so. Me, I've done nothing."

"But you will," Twain said.

"Where do I start?"

"Where you think you should. What you're thinking right now. Leave San Francisco, go up into the Gold Country, stay with a friend. And write. One story. That's all it takes. Write that one story. The rest will follow."

Joan wondered if Sam had had this idea and just

hadn't shared it with her and Lee. Or maybe Twain was giving Sam the idea right now for the first time. Either way, Joan knew Sam would soon be leaving San Francisco. It seemed like the right move.

"But Huck and Tom and all the rest," Sam said.

"One story. We have to start somewhere. You can't write an entire life's work in one day. Trust me, I'm living proof you'll write that story and more. Write the first one."

"Which one?"

"You'll find it," Twain said, "then write it."

"That simple?" Sam asked.

"Honor bright," Twain said.

Sam eased a bit.

"Look," Twain said, "I won't be here long. This unstuck business is as tricky as ever. The older I get, I find I have less time in each when I *visit*. I don't know why, rightly, just the way it is. The mysteries never cease. Any last questions?"

Joan couldn't help herself.

"Mr. Twain, sir," she said. "Does coming unstuck keep happening? I mean, will it always happen?"

"If you're lucky," Twain said. "Yes. If you remember what it's like. And call me Sam. I'm always Sam."

Joan hoped he was right.

"Lee?" Twain said. "Anything?"

"I'm cool, Sam," he said. And Joan saw that he was.

"Sam?" Twain asked. "Last chance. For now."

"Will I be happy?" Sam asked.

"Sometimes."

"Will I be sorrowful, too?"

"Sometimes."

"But—"

"Wait. It's a long journey. Save some surprises. Oh, well, good-bye."

Twain puffed up a cloud of story and words, and within that cloud, he began to fade, and then he was gone.

Or Is It the First? – The End of One Thing – The Beginning of Another

Sam sat by himself on the sofa, puffing on his pipe. Underneath all the smoke, he was laughing, his shoulders shaking. He was slapping his knee and bending over and trying to talk and waving his pipe about. He looked like he'd heard one of those jokes that starts out pretty funny but turns into a howler.

Lee and Joan looked at each other. WHAT THE HECK.

"Sam," Lee asked, "you okay?"

He nodded, wiping the tears from his eyes.

"Good," Joan said. "Now, put out your pipe. It's gross."

The hotel room had grown rather smoky. Lee went over to the windows and slipped them both open. The day was warm again. Indian Summer. 1864. It smelled great. Lee suddenly wanted to get out into it, the new day.

"Do you mind telling us what's so funny?" Joan asked.

She knew it had something to do with Twain, of course, but she hadn't expected laughter. Sam had been running from Twain for weeks.

He put away his pipe.

"Telling the truth," Sam said, "is the funniest joke in the world. It was so simple. I wanted my future so badly, but it terrified me. So I ran from it. And yet I've been telling you two all along, don't fret, go forth. People have endless fountains of advice for others, but when it comes to their own lives, the same fountain runs dry as a bone. If only I would listen to myself."

"You just did," Lee said.

"I know, right, dude?" Sam said it perfectly.

"Dude," Lee said.

"I kept thinking," Sam said, "that I had to do everything at once. Become Mark Twain instantly. Write *Huck* and *Tom* and everything else all in one sitting." He leaned back. "But all I have to do, it turns out, is take the first step. Write the first story."

"My, my," Joan said, "that sounds suspiciously like a lesson. A moral to the story."

Joan no longer believed what Sam had said, back on

the *Paul Jones*, about lessons and morals and how they could ruin an exciting adventure. She now firmly believed, from her own experience, that the best adventures offered you lessons, no matter what. If not, an adventure was just a roller-coaster ride. An amusement. A true adventure, Joan realized, took you places—or times—you could not have begun to imagine. Always something to be learned in the unknown.

"Perhaps," Sam said, nodding quietly. "Perhaps."

The smoke was clearing. Lee and Joan both felt that something had ended.

Everyone, Sam included, sat back and took in the moment. Breathed. OKAY.

Lee heard these words in his brain: The ending has ended; it is time for the beginning to begin.

"What will you do, Sam?" Lee asked.

"I'll do what I told myself to do. I'll go up into the hills, and I'll write a story. The first one. And then I'll write another, I suppose."

"And what do *we* do, Sam?" Joan wanted to know. She felt a scratch of fear in her voice. She knew that a new journey was just starting, but how to do that? The future was still so unpredictable moment by moment. And part of her wasn't ready to go. It was always hard to leave.

"Go home, I imagine," Sam said. "Each of you has your own first step to take into the future."

"Be careful," Joan said. "I smell another lesson coming."

"Bother lessons," Sam said. "Cast off."

The unanimous decision is the only kind of decision for a group of travelers to make. Anything less leaves at least one disgruntled traveler, and that's all it takes to ruin a journey. Everyone—Sam and Lee and Joan—suspected that Fort Point, once again, was a good enough destination. Each of them claimed to have a mild case of arm fish, that tingling. Might as well.

They each voiced some concern about the butchers. Shouldn't they be worried about them, those cleavers? Sam put forth the argument that last night's party on the *Paul Jones*, and the strict chaperoning by the Misses Greta and Penelope and their shotguns, had undoubtedly sent the butchers home, tails between legs.

"Cowards are like that," Sam said. "Cowardly. They prefer the cover of night. Besides, if we can stand up to our future selves, we can stand down some butchers."

Sam ran downstairs and ordered eggs and bacon and biscuits and gravy from the hotel's kitchen, while

Joan and Lee stared out the window at the crowds on Market Street. They were trying to remember everything they were seeing.

The breakfast, all agreed, was fit for kings and queens. No, they re-agreed, not even kings and queens. No one had ever, in any time or place, enjoyed such a fine meal.

Into the soldier's backpack, Lee put his *Starcruiser Omega,* Joan her letter and book. Souvenirs from the past and the future.

When they stepped out into Market Street's high warm day, they all turned their faces to the sun. There was no menace in this day. A fine carriage awaited.

Mostly they were quiet during the carriage ride to Fort Point. Out of downtown to the bay, past Meiggs' Wharf and the Pioneer Woolen Mills, the travelers pulled into their own thoughts.

Joan knew it was time to get home again, but she was reluctant to leave Sam. If that's what was actually going to happen.

Lee didn't want to leave Sam, ever, but he was ready to return to 2012.

The turning of the carriage wheels over the rugged road, that was the only sound.

When the carriage reached the seawall road that led to Fort Point, Sam banged on the roof with his hand, and the driver stopped.

"We should walk from here," Sam said.

And it felt like the right thing to do. So they did it.

They got out of the carriage and walked along the seawall road. Fort Point waited ahead.

"It's been bugging me," Lee said. "Why here, to come unstuck? Why Fort Point, why the lighthouse? That part's still a little nutty."

"I've thought mightily on this," Sam said. "Think of where the lighthouse stands. The Golden Gate is on the border between east and west, between yesterday, the sun setting, and today, the sun rising. It is on the cusp of the oldest part of the world, China, and the newest part, San Francisco. And it is on the farthest edge of San Francisco itself, which is where people come to find whole new futures."

Both Lee and Joan wanted to say something more. Silence seemed wrong. Lee asked the only question he could dredge up.

"Do we know this will work?" he asked. "Do we know this is the way home?"

Lee thought Sam would answer his question. But it was Joan.

"Feel it, Lee?" she said. "Those tingly arm fish?"

Joan expected Lee to say "but" or something.

"Yeah," was all he said. "Just checking."

Fort Point was just ahead of them. Lee turned to look

back at San Francisco, and there it was in all its 1864 glory, the Pioneer Woolen Mills puffing black smoke into the beautiful day. Joan looked, too.

When they turned back around, surprisingly the fog was drifting in and around the towers of the Golden Gate Bridge. The school buses in the Fort Point parking lot were yellow smudges.

Oh, they both thought, that was easy. And they expected that when they turned around again, towards downtown, that Sam and 1864 would be gone.

They turned together.

But Sam was still there and so was 1864. Half of the world was in fog, half in sun.

Joan and Lee turned one way, then another: The past, the future; the future, the past. And there, in between, were the three Unstuckians.

Sam was looking around, too. "Cool, dudes," was what Sam said. "This is so totally freakin' cool."

Joan knew what Lee was thinking, and Lee knew what Joan was thinking. They were thinking the same thing.

They looked at each other. THE HARD PART.

"Sam," Joan asked, "will we see you again? Ever?"

"Only time will tell," he said.

Sam shook their hands.

It was all they could do, all they could say.

"Later, dudes," Sam said, and he turned around and walked back to the waiting carriage.

Lee and Joan watched him for a little while, but it was too hard. As one, they turned and headed back to Fort Point, to 2012, to now.

Lee snuck a peek behind him. Joan snuck a peek, too. Sam was gone. The city was its 2012 self again, all buildings and freeways and noise.

The City School eighth graders were getting back onto the buses. The field trip was over.

Lee and Joan looked at each other and shrugged—the old NO WAY shrug. They knew they might get into some kind of trouble for missing the buses back to school, but there was no real reason to get on those buses. There was nothing there for them any longer, so they turned around.

They walked back along the seawall road, passing under the freeway, then cut up the hill into the Presidio. For a long time, they walked in silence through 2012. Lee shouldered the backpack for a while, then Joan took it from him, her turn. Together they stared at the Civil War backpack. Great souvenir.

Overhead, the day could not make up its mind, sunny and foggy all at once.

They knew where they were going. They were headed back home—first Joan's, then Lee's. It would be good to be home.

Yes, they knew where they were going. And *when*. Now.